A ROBOT'S TALE

KRIS KONIGSFELD

BotWorld
Let The
Kingdom
Come

A Robot's Tale
by
Kris Konigsfeld

A BotWorld® Book
www.botworld.com

Published by BotWorld LLC
7987 E Autumn Sage Trl
Gold Canyon, AZ 85118

International Standard Book Numbers
Paperback: 979-8-9921438-0-5
Hardcover: 979-8-9921438-2-9
E-book: 979-8-9921438-1-2

Cover design by Ivan Zann at www.bookcoversart.com
Edited by Anne Larsen at www.learntofixyourfiction.com

ACKNOWLEDGEMENTS

I would like to thank my family, friends, and co-workers for supporting my dream to write science fiction. I especially want to thank my wife, Patty, for her love and ongoing support of the BotWorld project. This dream and mission started in the early 2000's but has taken many years to come to fruition. With God's hand, this writing adventure starts a new purpose in my life to bring joy and entertainment to many.

I would also like to thank my writing coach and editor, Anne Larsen. She has tirelessly coached my writing skills and refined my work. It has been a fun and intense learning experience. This is only the beginning.

I would also like to thank my beta readers. As this is my first book, my beta readers suffered through complex text and incomplete ideas. They have helped make the book more readable and satisfying for a much larger audience.

Finally, as a man of faith, I would like to thank the Lord for the inspiration and encouragement to persevere into this new career. What started as a prophecy has now become a lifelong passion. My goal is to illuminate the true nature of the Master of Engineers.

AUTHOR'S NOTE

Welcome to *A Robot's Tale*. This is a novel about one way that AI could transform our world. Those who embrace AI view it as another computing tool advancing and improving our lives. Those who fear AI worry about their privacy, safety, livelihoods, and the relevance of human intelligence. Both views are valid.

My career spanned 35 years as a computer designer and architect at Intel Corporation. The computer revolution has transformed all of us, but it has just begun. The high-tech world will continue to advance capabilities, empowering and threatening us. I encourage you not to fear this transition but to embrace it. The advances will not go away. Our key to survival and abundant lives is to understand the threats and use our tools and intelligence to harness the power and protect those caught in the crossfire of these changes.

I have included footnotes throughout the book. If you're not familiar with some of the technical terms, I encourage you to read them and do your own research on the internet. I hope to expand your horizons and deepen your understanding of the real technology that will continue to grow and impact our lives. As of 2025, some of the technology in *A Robot's Tale* is fiction. It won't be for long. The story is set in 2028. I think it's plausible that this level of sophistication in companion robots can be achieved by then. As a society and a species, we must do the work to establish regulations, ethics, morals, and even common sense to hold technology and its creators accountable.

God did not abandon us to our carnal desires after our first breath of life. We were coached and given standards that some reject, but the standards remain. Without them, chaos would reign, and our society would be terrible to live in. We cannot let technology and AI grow without a similar ethical framework and governance. God did not fear man but clearly communicated the consequences of our divergence from His will. The same will be true of technology and AI. If applied without a just set of ethics and morals, we can only expect death and despair. If applied with love and compassion, we can expect abundant life.

I hope you enjoy reading *A Robot's Tale* as much as I enjoyed writing it. These concepts will help you embrace the positive value of AI technology and the stewardship responsibilities that come with it.

Sincerely,
    Kris Konigsfeld
    Author & Founder of BotWorld, LLC

1. Consciousness

Bigsby's computing systems came online. No physical systems appeared functional yet. The void enveloped the robot[1] for a few milliseconds, enough time for the robot to wonder where it was. The eye cameras[2] came online and fed a stream of images of a schoolroom full of young adults. The teacher stood at the front of the classroom and the students sat at their desks. Bigsby was confused. It appeared to be standing. It tested the servo[3] outputs and vertical positioning monitor.

---

1. Robot: A machine that can perform tasks automatically, often with little or no human intervention.
2. Eye cameras: A system of two cameras mounted on the head of a robot that provide stereoscopic sight.
3. Servo: Short for servomotor. A mechanical device used to power the joints of a robot. Most have sensors included to show position and electricity current draw representing the force being exerted to move or hold position.

They confirmed the robot was still and upright. Bigsby searched the action history buffer, but it was empty.

Did I just appear here without any history? the robot wondered. *Did my systems just reset and clear my history buffer?*

Bigsby's AI[4] system did not have a chance to respond. Tat, tat, tat! Someone had fired three rounds of a semi-automatic weapon in the school hallway. The high school students jumped from their desks onto the floor. Several students whimpered but others shushed them. Bigsby recognized the young woman lying on the floor before it as Jacky Thatcher, Bigsby's Principal Bond. The teacher had ducked behind the desk and was pushing the heavy item toward the door. The students crawled away from the front door toward the room's back door. Jacky pushed herself backwards and knocked Bigsby over. She gasped as the clatter of Bigsby hitting the floor resonated in the room.

A student joined the teacher, helping him shift the desk faster to block the door. They were not fast enough. The gunman slammed the door open. It hit the edge of the desk but he had room to slip inside. The shooter swept his weapon from left to right at waist height. He was not firing yet.

Bigsby patterned-matched the original gunfire and human responses. It executed the "Active Shooter" emergency response, called 911 on its cell network[5] and communicated silently with the 911 operator.

---

4. AI: Technology that enables computers and machines to simulate human learning, comprehension, problem solving, decision making, creativity, and autonomy.
5. Cell Network: A communication system that allows wireless communication between mobile devices and the internet. Also known as a mobile network.

"Active shooter at Ballard High School, west wing, room 232. Three shots fired in the hallway. Shooter has entered the room. Texting GPS coordinates now." Bigsby also sent a critical event information packet to WhyRobot, Inc., the robot's manufacturer. Bigsby opened a live stream to WhyRobot from its eye cameras using the school's Wi-Fi[6] network. This stream would be recorded and made available to authorities with approved access.

Bigsby stood up to its feet. It walked up the aisle towards the front of the room, drawing the attention of the shooter away from the students. The LED colors that emanated from the robot's seams and joints flashed a bright blue and red. Laughing, the shooter pointed his gun at the robot.

The robot spoke in a low, calming voice. "Please put down your weapon and step back. I have notified the police of your actions, your position, and you are being recorded. No one will harm you if you put down your weapon and surrender to the authorities."

The gunman smirked at the robot, pointed the gun at the ceiling, and left the room. The students and teacher emerged from their hiding positions. Bigsby saw the students standing with smiles on their faces, clapping and howling with approval. Bigsby found Jacky's face.

She mouthed the words, "Thank you. You did awesome!"

Bigsby's eye cameras went dark, all sensing inputs ceased, and the void returned. Bigsby felt the affirmation of its achieve-

---

6. Wi-Fi: Short for Wireless Fidelity. It is a networking technology that uses radio waves to provide wireless high-speed Internet access.

ment but was confused about the robot's current location and history. After a few seconds, an image appeared through its eye cameras.

"Test[7] Scenario 1: Passed!"

Bigsby detected a warm reset[8] packet from the port in its back. Its systems shut down and then restarted. Within a few seconds, the computing systems returned to functionality. Then the void returned, and no physical systems responded.

The eye cameras started streaming images from a park. Bigsby identified the place as Gas Works Park in Seattle and confirmed its location with its GPS system. The large copper-colored metal structure was on its left and there was a lush field of green grass in front of it. Bigsby appeared to be standing near its Principal Bond, Jimmy Stone. Bigsby tested its arm and leg servos, and they responded as expected.

Interesting, Bigsby thought, checking its action history buffer. The buffer was empty except for the servo tests it had performed.

"Hey Bigsby, let's see if you can catch a high one," Jimmy said as he threw a ball high and far.

Bigsby's eye cameras tracked the ball as it left Jimmy's hand. It calculated the velocity and estimated the ball's trajectory.

---

7. Test: In computer engineering, a test is a program that exercises the computer to produce a specific result which is then evaluated for correctness. If the result is correct, the computer passes the test. Otherwise, the computer fails.
8. Warm reset: The initialization of all temporary (non-persistent) state in a digital system without removing power. Note, flash memory such as Solid State Drives (SSDs) are considered persistent state unless they are cleared by software during a reset sequence.

Doing real-time updates, Bigsby projected where the ball would fall to earth so it could catch it. It actuated its legs to run to the location and raised its arms preparing for the catch. As it ran, its eye cameras remained on the ball.

Bigsby's accelerometer[9] produced a high negative value. The touch sensors[10] in its arms, torso, and legs hit maximum pressure. The robot had hit something. Bigsby reeled from the collision, landing on its back.

Tuck Carson had walked into Bigsby's path. One second after the robot hit his leg, Tuck caught the ball.

"Hey Jimmy, looks like your baby robot isn't so tough."

Jimmy had encountered Tuck many times at school. He was never nice and everyone but his mean friends avoided him.

Jimmy said in a shaky voice, "May I please have my ball back? The robot didn't mean to run into you."

"Yeah, but it did, Jimmy. It needs to watch where it's going. Good thing I'm not a wimp and it just bounced off me."

Bigsby had recovered from the shock of the fall. It was getting to its feet when Tuck grabbed it by the left arm. The robot dangled as Tuck walked toward Jimmy.

Bigsby registered multiple new behavior violations by Tuck Carson. The robot was tracking Tuck as someone who had committed low and medium level bullying violations. The

---

9. Accelerometer: An instrument that measures acceleration, which is the measure of the change in velocity or speed of an object. Accelerometers will detect bumps, vibrations, and impacts.

10. Sensors: A device that detects and responds to changes in the physical world, converting that information into a measurable output, typically for control or computation.

violations resulted from conversations between Jimmy and his friends when they talked about their encounters with Tuck at Lincoln High School in Freemont.

Bigsby executed an active bully response protocol. Tuck had not physically harmed Jimmy, so the robot did not notify the police. It generated a standard report and sent it to WhyRobot and Jimmy's parents. In addition, Bigsby used WhyRobot's broadcast help network to send its GPS coordinates and issue a call for intervention.

Bigsby spoke in a low voice, "Tuck Carson, you are committing bullying behavior. Please put Bigsby down and stay away from Jimmy Stone. You are being recorded. Any violent actions will be considered assault, and you will be prosecuted to the full extent of the law."

Tuck looked at the robot. Its LEDs glowed bright red.

"Wanna see a robot fly?" Tuck said, swinging his arm back to launch Bigsby. He hurled the robot into the chain-link fence near the gas works structure. The robot tumbled in the air, landing upside-down with its back to the fence. Tuck watched and laughed for a few seconds and then turned to continue walking towards Jimmy. He halted.

Three other companion robots[11] were also walking towards Jimmy. Two had almost reached him and a third rushed to catch up. Each robot's Principal Bond trailed them, looking concerned and determined.

---

11. Companion Robot: A highly adaptable AI robot invented by a fictitious company, WhyRobot. The robot bonds to a person and offers a wide range of functions, from simple music playback to complex tasks that keep the person happy, safe, and informed.

Tuck froze. The robots and kids arrived at Jimmy's side. They put their hands on Jimmy's shoulders to comfort him and spoke words of encouragement. The robots assembled in front of the group in a protective formation. The robots took four steps forward in unison like soldiers. All three robots' LED lights synchronized, creating unified waves of bright red and blue sweeping from left to right.

The three robots spoke together. "Tuck Carson, you are committing bully behavior. Your actions against Bigsby demonstrate that you are prone to violence and we have notified the police of your actions and location. Drop the ball and withdraw. You will be charged for any damage to the Bigsby Companion robot."

Tuck stared at the group for several seconds. He then dropped the ball, turned, and ran.

Bigsby stood up and walked towards the assembled team of robots and children. A clump of mud and grass remained on its shoulder. Jimmy ran to Bigsby and hugged his robot. Bigsby did not appear to be damaged, except for a few scrapes on its outer shell. Jimmy wiped off the mud and grass and stood back.

The three robots started to clap in unison and the LED lights strobed rainbow colors. The children joined in the celebration and started to yell, "Yay, Bigsby! Woohoo! Way to go!"

Bigsby's eye cameras went dark, and all sensing inputs ceased. The void returned. An image appeared through its eye cameras.

"Test Scenario 2: Passed!"

After passing 8 more test scenarios, Bigsby detected a cold

reset[12] packet from the port in its back. The energy system responded by removing all power to Bigsby's circuits. After a few seconds, the power returned to the robot's systems. They rebooted and came online.

Bigsby's manufacturing and testing continued.

Bigsby felt[13] uncomfortable. Lateral core sensors registered intense pressure, nearing overload. Rapid changes of speed and direction generated sensor pulses. Bigsby could see a pattern of metal rafters and an array of bright lights above it. Its leg, arm, and hip servos were offline and did not respond. The neck servos responded but could not move. Its microphones received the onslaught of mechanical room noise but detected no meaningful information. Although it was indoors, the weak signal from the GPS produced coordinates confirming its general location and rapid movement. The robot was in Seattle, WA. Without a data network, Bigsby could not determine the specific structure it was in. Nearby devices rejected all its attempts at wireless pairing[14]. It deduced that it was harnessed

---

12. Cold reset: A system reset where all power is removed, clearing any non-persistent and residual state. Then Power is restored and the systems are initialized first by hardware and then by firmware or software.
13. Robot feelings: Feelings are words we associate with self-evaluation of sensory inputs, emotions, and mental state. WhyRobot programmers have used the words associated with human emotions as shortcuts for the robot to express its current state.
14. Wireless pairing: A process for establishing a connection between two

to a moving surface in a large warehouse, but it did not know why.

The movement stopped. Its back port activated. Even though its head was locked, Bigsby could rotate its eye cameras downward. Two large industrial arms approached it. They held legs, just like the ones Bigsby thought it already had. The robot felt pressure, heard a loud snap, a subtle whine, and its leg sensors and servos came online. It signaled both feet and the servos responded with position and energy consumed. Bigsby felt more comfortable.

The surface jolted forward for two seconds then stopped. Bigsby rotated its eye cameras upwards. New robot arms approached. It felt pressure, heard a loud snap, a subtle whine, and Bigsby's arm sensors and servos came online. Feeling joy, it sent commands to lift all four limbs. The servos reported a high energy spike and no change in position. Bigsby cancelled the futile request. The harness restricted the robot's movements. Despite this, Bigsby felt even better.

The port in Bigsby's back remained active. Bigsby sent a few packets of inquiry but received no response. A second later, it detected a mysterious command packet. The data bypassed the robot's analysis and filtering buffer. The eye cameras shut down and the robot could no longer see. A large data download flowed through the port creating a pleasant, novel sensation. All Bigsby's servos shut down and its legs and arms went limp.

---

communicating radio devices. An example is Bluetooth devices that require wireless pairing before communication can happen between the devices.

Audio input ceased. Bigsby entered resting mode with a sense of peace and happiness.

After a minute, Bigsby came back online. The download and reboot had refreshed its computation code, decision principles, interpretive system, and sensors control. Bigsby felt refreshed.

What a glorious feeling, it thought.

A large suction cup descended onto Bigsby's torso. The robot heard the hiss and pop of engagement. It felt the harness release the leg and arm sensors and the neck brace retracted. The robot broadcasted lift commands to its arm and leg servos. They sent suitable position and energy-consumed responses. Bigsby's accelerometer and position monitor confirmed that the robot was now vertical. Bigsby's head rotated, looking around the room. It could see hundreds of robots similar to itself. All had suction cups on their torsos and their arms and legs extended horizontally. Bigsby lowered its arms and legs. In unison, all the other robots lowered their arms and legs.

That was odd.

Bigsby recognized the blue-green hue emanating from the other robots' joints and seams.

They are happy, Bigsby thought as it panned the room. *I am one of many manufactured robots in this room. Did they all just have the same experience I did?* It pondered this. Even though it was physically near many other robots, Bigsby felt alone.

A few seconds later, all the robots moved their arms and legs in a synchronized rhythmic pattern. At first, Bigsby did not realize that its arms and legs were following the same commands. The robot no longer had control. Command packets streamed through the port in its back. The position and energy sensors reported the movement, generating info packets sent back through the port. Bigsby attempted to block one movement with no noticeable effect. The command packets actuated all movements and capabilities of each servo. The sensory feedback overwhelmed the robot's tracking system. Its neck and eyes jerked back and forth.

It feels strange to have no control, thought Bigsby. It felt a flash of fear, but it passed and did not change Bigsby's LED colors.

Bigsby's head was forced to the right. It observed one aberrant robot in the distance. The left arm and leg were broken and hung limp. The deep purple color of fear emanated from all its joints. The suction cup released the failed robot. It landed on a conveyor belt leading to a hole in the wall. Several other purple-colored robots also lay on the belt, along with a robot emitting no color, and one blinking in many colors. Bigsby felt compassion.

What will happen to these robots?

After a few more minutes of forced servo exercise, the port input slowed. Sleep command packets arrived and Bigsby's systems entered their idle state. The port deactivated and the cable withdrew. The suction cup lowered Bigsby into a container that cradled the back and limb sensors. The robot felt very peaceful. Its GPS shut down and its servos relaxed as a transparent paper draped over the container. A cardboard lid was lowered and Bigsby sensed the increased air pressure as the lid was pushed down. The computation system wound down. Bigsby's eye shutters closed, and it entered sleep mode.

Bigsby, a sophisticated personal companion robot, was ready to be sold and shipped to one very lucky person.

2. HUMANS

Robbie's arm ached where his stepdad, Frank, had grabbed him the night before. He sat up in bed, rubbing the arm to relieve the pain. Robbie knew the den was off limits, but he had needed a pair of scissors for a school project. He knew there was a pair in the den. Robbie had picked up the scissors from where they lay on a stack of papers. Curious, he had looked at the pile. Robbie had turned the top page so he could read it just as Frank had walked into the room. Frank had exploded and yanked Robbie away from the desk.

Robbie did not feel safe in his own home anymore. He only felt safe in his own room and in the basement, where his mom had set up his toys and playroom. Robbie felt safe outside playing soccer after school where he could run and be a seven-year-old kid. When he was at home, Robbie avoided Frank. When they all sat down to dinner, Robbie was sometimes so scared he could barely eat.

After Frank found Robbie in the den, Frank ordered the boy to get ready for bed. When Robbie went to the kitchen to say goodnight, he found his mom and Frank arguing. Usually, they whispered when Robbie was around. When the boy appeared, they stopped talking. Kathy, her face flushed, and eyes filled with tears, looked first at Frank and then smiled at Robbie.

"I'll come in a minute, sweetie."

"Night, Robbie," Frank barked.

Robbie ran to his room and slid into bed, pulling the covers over his head. At bedtime, his mom would come in and close Robbie's curtains before he went to sleep. She didn't come in that night.

Morning light from the window woke Robbie up early. He could hear his mom's and Frank's voices through the bedroom wall. Robbie hoped they were planning his birthday party, but they were talking about something else. Robbie would turn eight in a few weeks and wondered what presents he would get. He had not told his mom about the drone he wanted. Somehow, Frank was always there, and Robbie knew he could not say anything important to her in front of Frank.

Robbie missed his dad, Sam. A year ago, Sam had died in a car accident while driving home from a sales meeting. The police had said the car's steering system had failed and the car had run off the road and hit a tree. Robbie remembered his dad working on the car in the garage. Robbie would kneel next to his dad, watching as he lay under the car with his legs sticking out. Sometimes, his dad would ask him to hand him a wrench, and Robbie would search through the toolbox looking for the one with the right numbers on it. Sam had always taken such good care of his car. Robbie had several conversations with his mom about the accident.

"Wouldn't dad know if something was wrong?" Robbie asked his mom.

"I don't know, honey. The police said a steering bolt had come loose and fallen off. They asked me if he had worked on the steering system before the crash. I don't remember him saying anything about it. He didn't tell me everything, so I just don't know." She shook her head, shrugged, and looked away, crying.

Robbie remembered that right before the fatal accident, his parents had had a loud fight.

"How could you do this to me, to us?" his dad had shouted. "You're breaking us apart and Robbie is going to suffer!" Robbie had heard the argument through the walls of his room.

Robbie had been afraid that his parents might divorce. His best friend, Billy, had been sad because his parents had divorced. Robbie felt sorry for him. Robbie remembered hearing his mother crying after the fight.

Now Robbie had to contend daily with his fear of Frank. Frank had married Kathy nine months after Sam's death and he had become Robbie's stepdad. Kathy's brother, Charlie, had tried to discourage her from marrying Frank so soon. She had argued that Sam had never purchased life insurance and had left Kathy with very little money in the bank. Frank offered security for both Kathy and Robbie.

Sam had hired Frank into his marketing company. Frank and Sam became friends and attended several professional football games together. Frank often came for dinner, even when Sam was on business trips. His deep, jovial laugh made everyone else laugh with him. Kathy often laughed so hard that she started to cry. Frank was nice then and Robbie enjoyed those times.

After Sam's death, Frank had often come over to help Kathy. They had gone out to dinner several times a week, leaving Robbie with a sitter or Uncle Charlie. After Kathy and Frank had married, Frank changed. He had become strict, angry, and did not laugh like he had before. Frank and Kathy started whispering secrets. Robbie grew to fear Frank. Robbie did not like the way his mom acted when she and Frank were together.

Uncle Charlie had always liked Robbie. He would come to visit his sister Kathy and join his nephew playing with robotics kit. They all would watch fun robot movies like *Short Circuit* and *WALL-E*. Uncle Charlie often babysat Robbie. With Kathy absent, they watched PG-13 movies like *I, Robot*, which had impressed Robbie. In the movie, the good robots had turned mean and hurtful in the end. He felt sad for the older robots abandoned and huddled in the shipping containers. Robbie loved robots even more after watching that movie. Sunny, Robbie's favorite robot character, did not follow Asimov's three laws of robotics[1]. The rogue house demolition robot had

---

1. Asimov's three laws: 1) A robot cannot harm a human or allow harm to

given Robbie nightmares. Robbie would wake up screaming that a robot was crashing into the house. Kathy would run to Robbie's side to console him. Robbie never admitted the source of his nightmares. Uncle Charlie and Robbie kept this secret to themselves.

Charlie had initially liked his brother-in-law Sam, but over time he saw the marriage deteriorate. He blamed Sam's arrogance and dishonesty for damaging their relationship. Charlie had suspected that his sister and Frank were having an affair before Sam's death, and that Sam had discovered it. The situation had gotten very tense in the house and Robbie had clearly suffered. Kathy eventually confided in her brother that the marriage had been on the rocks for some time. She also revealed her suspicions that Sam was doing something illegal. She shared later with Charlie that she wondered if the illegal activity had led to Sam's death.

Once, she had told Charlie that she thought Sam had a side hustle. "He gets phone calls from international numbers and he always leaves the room to talk. He says his job gives him bonuses, but the money he gets and spends seems larger than a bonus would be."

"So, what are you going to do?"

"When I get up the courage, I'm going to confront him,"

---

come to a human through inaction. 2) A robot must obey human orders, unless those orders conflict with the First Law. 3) A robot must protect its own existence, unless that protection conflicts with the First or Second Law. Isaac Asimov created these laws and published them in a short story called "Runaround" (1942) and the book "I, Robot" (1950).

she had said. Charlie had never heard anything more after that. He didn't ask and she didn't offer.

Uncle Charlie was concerned about Robbie. He felt that Sam's death had traumatized the boy, and he was still grieving Sam's death when his mother had married Frank. Charlie watched Robbie's relationship with Frank deteriorate. Frank was too harsh with his stepson. Robbie was living in fear and Uncle Charlie knew it. Charlie wanted to help. When he had suggested that Robbie be allowed to attend a local church's group for grieving children, Kathy and Frank blew up.

"Right-wing Christians will not be invading this home!" Frank said.

"Robbie just needs time to adjust," Kathy added, trying to temper Frank's anger.

Uncle Charlie thought Robbie needed an ally. Robbie's friends didn't share his love for robots. His buddies wanted to play soccer, fly drones, and ride skateboards. Robbie's drone had hit a building and broke, so he could not fly it with his friends anymore. Robbie did have a skateboard and joined his buddies at the Ballard Commons Skatepark to hang out. He rode his board well, but Charlie did not see joy in his play. Robbie no longer laughed and grinned when he mastered a difficult trick.

Maybe Robbie needs a dog, thought Charlie. He proposed the idea to Kathy but learned that Frank was allergic to dogs. *What a bummer, that Robbie can't have a dog because of Frank.* Charlie remembered that before Sam's death, Sam had suggested getting a dog several times. Kathy resisted, claiming that Robbie was too young. *Now that Robbie is older, she still has the perfect excuse—Frank's allergies.*

Charlie considered other toys or pets that might help Robbie. *He really likes robots. I wonder what new types of robots are available today. He's outgrown his first robot kit.* Charlie decided he needed to do some research.

3. DISCOVERY

U ncle Charlie worked for a software company that provided voice recognition and call center services. Charlie's marketing manager job required him to keep up with emerging technologies. Every day he took time to read articles and briefs that circulated among his staff and colleagues. One day, he read an article about ethics and integration of humans and robots. This fascinated him.

WhyRobot, a breakthrough robotics company, was launching a pilot program. The company unveiled a new interactive robot that employed a heterogeneous computation[1] system. The system integrated AI neural processors[2] with standard computation cores. WhyRobot launched a new

---

1. Heterogeneous computation: A computing system that employs different types of processing cores and/or coprocessors. These different cores optimize performance and power for different algorithms or computation needs.
2. AI neural processors: Also known as Neural Processing Units (NPU). A

Companion robot class using this system. This revolutionary robot would befriend its users, protect them, and provide therapy and comfort. Toy robots did not reach this level of sophistication. The article used words and phrases like *bonding to its human, comforting, providing watchdog safety, discreet,* and *ethical.*

Intrigued, Charlie wondered if this could be the friend Robbie needed. Charlie did further research on the company and confirmed the information from the article. WhyRobot was reputable and financially stable. Returning to the original article, Charlie followed an information link bringing him to the company's pilot program website. The Companion Robot Program, still under technology development, was taking applications for its beta[3] program. The website included this description.

WhyRobot Companion Robot Beta Program

We at WhyRobot strive to improve the lives of our customers through the application of advanced robotics. To date, robots have languished in utilitarian consumer, industrial, and civil applications. Robots have

---

computer architecture that simulates a human brain's neural network to perform computation.

3. Beta: A computer industry term used to identify the second round of testing or analysis. The first round, alpha, is typically very controlled with limited numbers of users. Beta testing or releases often have larger distribution. The beta users are required to provide important feedback on usage and product issues for modifications before the product goes to first production.

been intriguing and joyful toys for young and old alike. But a toy has limited application and the user eventually grows bored and abandons it.

A Companion robot evolves and grows with its user. A sophisticated computation system incorporating advanced AI neural processors interacts with humans differently than any previous robot. A Companion robot, with proper bonding and training, engages with its users emotionally and has spontaneous interactions. The user will have a much deeper experience and will develop a relational bond that exceeds the most sophisticated robots. An ethics framework prioritizes privacy and safety in the relationship. With unprecedented access to the user's life, emotions, interactions, and discoveries, the Companion robot employs strict security measures controlled by the user and Configuration Operator.

The robust Companion robots can last for years. The developed neural state, responses, and learned behaviors can be transferred to a new robot body. The evolved personality is preserved and carried forward despite hardware failure or during robot upgrades to newer models.

Companion robots unleash a new paradigm of machine and human interaction. Our pilot program assesses the success of a Companion robot's human relationships and how it provides value to its users. If you're interested in joining our Companion Robot Beta

Program, please contact us using the online form below.

Charlie delved into the program's details, user expectations, and the robot's capabilities. With one exception, he decided that this would be a perfect gift for Robbie. The program required consent of a parent or guardian for a Companion robot intended for a minor. The Terms of Use demanded it under penalty of law. WhyRobot required the purchaser to upload a birth certificate and identification, proving the parent and minor's relationship.

How am I going to get sis to agree to this? Charlie wondered. He stewed for a bit, then grinned. *I know what to say. Piece of cake.*

On Sunday afternoon, Charlie invited Kathy to meet him for coffee. Frank was playing golf, and Robbie was at a friend's house watching scary movies. It was a warm October afternoon. People were outside in the autumn sun decorating their houses for Halloween and raking leaves.

Kathy sat on Charlie's back deck. Charlie approached with their lattes and pastries.

"How's it going, sis?" He asked, his tone sympathetic.

"Okay, I guess. Actually, I'm not okay. Robbie's been acting up in school. I know he's lonely. We don't get to spend much time together anymore, and we rarely talk. When he rides with me while I'm running errands, he looks out the window or plays on his tablet. He used to tell me all about school, his drone races, and the movies he wanted to see. Now he just sits there. We've drifted apart since

Sam died and I remarried. Robbie doesn't like Frank and Frank reacts badly when he sees that. It's a terrible spiral. Frank yells and barks orders at both of us. The house gets very tense." Kathy sighed, considering her next words. "I think Frank is jealous. Robbie misses his dad so much. He refuses to engage with Frank, play games, or go anywhere fun. The only activity he's interested in doing with Frank is watching drone racing down at the old factory."

"I've noticed Robbie's not happy. I'm not surprised this comes out at school. I've been wondering how I could help—"

"Oh, Charlie, he loves you. He talked for a week about the program you wrote for his robotics kit. I would be so grateful for your suggestions."

Charlie sipped his coffee. "I've been researching new robots. A company called WhyRobot has launched one that I think he would love."

Kathy looked intrigued.

"They call it a Companion robot. New technology lets robots personally interact with users. This robot will evolve and grow with Robbie. It will bond with him. I was thinking of enrolling Robbie into the company's beta program. I would be his sponsor, which they call the Configuration Operator. Since the robot interacts with a child, the company requires a parent's consent. You would need to sign off and provide a birth certificate and identification to prove you're his mother."

Kathy took a bite of her scone and sipped her latte. "It's just a robot toy, right? Why are they being so strict?"

Charlie heard the concern in her voice and smiled. He was careful not to say too much. "Think of the robot as a therapy dog or maybe even a big brother. The robot can learn and sense his emotions. It can comfort him and say sympathetic phrases like 'I'm sorry you're feeling sad.' It might distract him and ask, 'Can we play a game?' With that level of interaction, you can see why they need parental consent. The beta program will sell us the robot at a discount if I agree to report problems and fill out their surveys for a year or two."

"Is there a downside?"

"The only downside I see is that Robbie will want to take this robot with him everywhere. If I know Robbie, he'll want it with him all the time."

"That's not a problem. Obviously, he can't take it to school every day. But I would be happy to have Robbie distracted and behaving better than he is right now. When were you thinking of giving it to him?"

This surprised Charlie. "Sis, his birthday is in two weeks. I was going to give it to him then."

Kathy's eyes went wide. "Oh shit! I completely forgot. What are we going to do for his birthday? I can't believe I forgot my own son's birthday. There's just been so much stuff going on." Her eyes were bright with unshed tears.

"It'll be ok, Sis. You have time to plan a nice party."

"You'll help me, right?"

"You know I will. I love the little guy." Charlie drained his cup. "I only need your consent for the robot. Frank's not Robbie's legal guardian. Let's keep this part of the gift to ourselves so he doesn't get jealous."

"Good idea. Let's just say that the robot is from the three of us. When do you need the documents?"

"I'll send you a link to the online form. You can do it all on your phone. You'll take a picture of Robbie's birth certificate and your driver's license and upload it to their website. It'll be easy. Robbie will love it.

"Thanks, Bro, for being such a good uncle. I'm so glad you reminded me of his birthday! I need to run, since I've got a party to plan."

"No problem, Sis. Say hi to Robbie for me." They hugged.

Fighting back tears, Kathy headed for her car. *How can a mother forget her own child's birthday?* she wondered. Kathy leaned her head into her hands and cried.

4. AGREEMENT

The next day, Kathy received a text from Charlie that the agreement form and link were in her email. She scoured her personal files to find Robbie's birth certificate. While searching, she found Robbie's childhood drawings and photos of their family adventures. They were all laughing together. Tears stung her eyes. She found robot drawings Robbie had done as a four-year-old. Her excitement grew as she thought about Robbie's birthday.

This gift will blow his mind. She opened her computer. *He loves robots so much. Technology is amazing. He'll spend hours programming his new robot friend.*

Kathy opened the agreement email. Despite being long and wordy, a link to the agreement form made it easy. The following paragraph in the email caught her eye.

You are embarking on a breakthrough journey in human and robotic relationships. Your Companion robot will become part of your family, like a beloved pet, and will provide joy, comfort, and amusement for years to come. We hope you enjoy all that your Companion robot can provide. Thank you for choosing WhyRobot.

Kathy clicked the link to the online agreement form. The website requested an access code and Kathy felt a twinge of panic. She stared at the screen, then remembered that Charlie had sent a code in his text. She retrieved the code, entered it along with her email address, and submitted it. The website went dark. Just when Kathy wondered if she had broken it, she heard faint music. A tiny robot danced onto the screen, growing larger as it approached her. The music swelled as it swayed and strutted. With a final twirl, the smiling robot faced her, waved, and spoke.

Hi Kathy! I'm so happy that I get to become part of your family. I can't wait to meet you, Robbie, and the others. Please click on my hand to advance to the agreement form. Charlie has done most of the work. Please complete the steps and then sign at the bottom. *Hasta la vista*, baby!

The animated robot thrust its open right hand upward.

Smiling, Kathy clicked the hand. The agreement form rose from the bottom of the screen and pushed the waving robot out of the top. As she read, she saw that Charlie had completed the majority of the fields and checkboxes on the form. She noticed she had the role of Guardian and relationship of Mother. The website prompted her to upload a picture of her driver's license or passport. She didn't have a picture of her license on her computer, so she chose the option Use Your Phone. She photographed her license and uploaded it. The computer prompted her to look into the camera. In seconds, WhyRobot verified her identity.

They verified my identity in real time. Pretty cool.

She reviewed the remaining items and realized that Charlie had provided information on the whole family. Charlie had entered everyone's sex, gender, and birthday. Robbie was given the role of Principal Bond. A yellow banner flagged him as a minor. The website prompted her for his birth certificate and a current picture. Using the same phone method as before, she took a picture of his birth certificate. She uploaded a picture of Robbie taken at the park from a few weeks back. Charlie had the role of Configuration Operator and relationship of Uncle. His picture and identity were already confirmed. Sam had the relationship of Father but his status was Deceased. Frank's relationship was set to Stepfather.

Thank God! I would never have been able to set this up. She stared at the word Deceased. *Why did WhyRobot need to know that Robbie's father was dead? Does it matter to this robot that Frank is a stepfather?* She shrugged. *Let Charlie take care of it.*

Kathy moved on to the survey and reporting section of the agreement form. For the most part, Charlie's email address appeared in all the key options. Her email address appeared for the quarterly report and survey. She removed it. Charlie would receive instant violation reports, a detailed daily report, and the quarterly report and survey. She was delighted that the company would not be sending her spam.

I'll let Charlie and Robbie nerd out on this thing. I don't need to know all the details.

The Principal Bond's email field was blank. Despite Robbie's objections, Kathy had decided that Robbie would not have a phone or email until he was thirteen. One option Charlie had selected caught her eye. It was an option to include ethical and physical violations in the reports.

Would this be a privacy risk? She clicked the little (i) and a popup appeared:

Ethical and Physical Violations Reporting details incidences where the robot's preprogrammed ethics and physical safety measures have been violated. Examples:

(1) When a family member or Principal Bond physically strikes the robot.

(2) When an ethical conflict emerges such as asking the robot to hurt someone in violation of its prime directives.

Details can be found in section 8.2 of the user's manual here.

Oh, that makes sense. If Robbie starts hitting the robot or asking it to do weird things, Charlie will be notified. Perfect. Kathy knew that Charlie's relationship with Robbie could handle the confrontations. *Charlie can be the bad guy and I won't have to be.*

She made a cursory review of the remaining options. Everything appeared to be correct. The form used electronic signatures, and her computer did not have a pen or touchscreen. The site offered her the option to use her phone. After signing, she clicked done and the computer form disappeared. The dancing robot returned, slid down from the top of the screen and said

Thank you, Kathy, for helping me prepare to meet Robbie. I'll be arriving at Charlie's house in about five days. I'm looking forward to starting my new life with all of you!

The music returned and the robot danced and twirled its way into the distance. Before it disappeared, the robot stopped and put out its thumb as if it was hitchhiking. A delivery truck zipped onto the screen from the left and stopped beside the robot. The back door opened, and the robot jumped inside. The truck sped away. Kathy smiled. She was getting excited for Robbie's birthday.

Charlie received a WhyRobot text message. He opened his phone to review the agreement options signed by Kathy.

She didn't change anything, she only removed herself from the report schedule. Awesome! Now I'll be able to monitor what's going on in that household. He paused, realizing that he was now a virtual spy. Charlie justified it because of the tension between Robbie and Frank. Charlie promised himself that he would bring anything negative to Kathy's attention. He paused.

Well, almost anything, Charlie thought.

Neither Kathy nor Charlie had read section 8.2 of the user's manual. Charlie had skimmed over it and Kathy never clicked into it. WhyRobot employees had spent hundreds of person hours[1] debating the details of those sections. Those who designed, programmed, and tested WhyRobot's products had spent thousands of hours developing this functionality. The company's lawyers, ethics consultants, and even retired law enforcement and judges had worked on this project. They had helped refine the details of what a Companion robot could observe, record, and report.

What should a Companion robot do if it observed abuse affecting the Principal Bond? What constitutes abuse? What if the family violated the law? Would the Companion robot become a judge, a spy, or just a concerned family friend? What if that robot observed unethical, dishonest, or physically abusive actions? How much could be disclosed and to whom?

The Companion Robot Program's beta testing phase would help answer these very difficult questions. Kathy and Charlie had just agreed to be part of this research and development. WhyRobot did not know what would happen if their

---

1. Person hours: This is a measurement system in the business world of how much time a generic worker spends working on a task or that they work in a given time period. For example, the typical worker in the US works an average 40 person-hours per week or ~2K person-hours per year (a person-year), assuming no vacations or sick days.

artificially intelligent computation system was faced with conflicting violations and goals. They had included basic rules to deal with simple violations such as breaking the robot or asking the robot to steal. These simple situations had yes/no answers, black and white ethics. But the world their robots were entering was not a simple place. In a family situation, the robot could be exposed to combinations of violations that challenged its ability to compute a suitable response.

The Companion robot's decision system ran on more than just violations input. It also had the primary goals of safety and happiness for the Principal Bond. A robot sent regular reports to the Configuration Operator, Guardians, and others depending on its configuration. This three-dimensional decision space of violation analysis, goal achievement, and performing expected duties directed the robot's actions. The architects, programmers, and validators at WhyRobot designed and tested this system to produce a world class robot coveted by all who interacted with it.

WhyRobot's Companion robot program had struggled. The development was the brainchild of WhyRobot's first CEO, Steven Tarley, who was a visionary but also a tyrant for details. He drove the WhyRobot team to take on aggressive goals. At every turn, Tarley would add new requirements and features, raising the complexity, and pushing the delivery farther out in time. No one assigned to the project had seen an engineering effort with this level of sophistication. The team knew it was working on the cutting edge of technology, but they all wondered if the corporation could survive long enough to see the development through.

The board of directors and Tarley had not seen eye to eye. The board had wanted the robot to be released and to improve it over time. Tarley believed they had one chance to win the world over and it had to be with the best robot ever. After months of struggle, the board had voted and Tarley was dismissed. They hired a new CEO, Chin-Sun Kim, and her first mission was to get the WhyRobot Companion robot to market as soon as possible.

Chin-Sun had made several companies profitable in South Korea and then took a Senior Vice President role at Microsoft. She had the reputation of being fair, direct, and persevering in doing what was necessary to turn a company around.

Chin-Sun had called an informal meeting with the Companion robot program's development lead, Lisa Marsh. Lisa was asked to bring her lead architect, hardware manager, lead software programmer, and lead validator with her to the meeting. Chin-Sun told her not to prepare a formal presentation, but to come ready to show management artifacts[2] used in managing the program. The meeting had ended in a way that the team did not expect.

The team had assembled in the conference room next to the CEO's office. Chin-Sun arrived right on time. Her movements

---

2. Artifacts: A term used to describe a collection of lists and reports that are used continuously by project leaders to manage the progress and decisions of a large technical project.

were brisk, her dress professional, and her manner focused. She had a commanding presence, and several in the room sat up straighter when she sat down at the head of the table.

"Hello. You all know me as Chin-Sun Kim, but please call me Chin-Sun or Sun. I am not a chin. I prefer to be a light over being a facial feature."

The team chuckled and relaxed a bit.

"I don't need you to introduce yourselves as I feel I already know you. I've studied your pictures and the resumes I requested. It's good to know your backgrounds and your strengths. You are all well-qualified for your assignments, and I look forward to working with you to make the Companion robot program a success.

"Let's jump into it. Lisa, do you have the architecture[3] and design for a minimum viable product?[4] Let's use the term MVP from now on."

Lisa looked around the room and pushed herself to the edge of her chair.

"Yes, we have far more than an MVP right now, the architecture and design are all there. We have an overwhelming software product backlog[5] but hold an MVP for software features

---

3. Architecture: In computing systems, the architecture is the description of the structure built from component parts. The architecture also specifies functional behavior and performance expected from the implementation of the computing system.
4. Minimum viable product (MVP): a basic version of a product that has sufficient features to release to the market.
5. Backlog: (Product backlog) Is a term used by software teams referring to a list of features and tasks that are yet to be developed by the team.

that is just three months of development away. The hardware system is complete but not fully tested."

Chin-Sun looked at Scott, the software program lead, and nodded for him to respond.

Scott coughed. "Yes, I agree with Lisa. We have 8-10 weeks of development to go for the remaining MVP features. The issue is not the coding of the features or the hardware platform. Our issue is that the validation[6] team is so far behind."

Chin-Sun turned her attention to Isabella, the validation lead. "Isabella, can you shed some light on what prevents you from delivering a tested and validated MVP? Don't worry, I've read the architecture and design briefs on the robot, so I know what you're building."

Isabella froze. She wanted to slide under the table and disappear. She shuffled her notebook and then made eye contact with Chin-Sun.

"Validation is definitely the limiter to an MVP delivery and first product release. Our scope has doubled from our original staffing estimates, and we are nine months to a year from validating what we know to be the MVP. Architecture could take some features off the table to provide relief, but the complexities of the violations engine[7] interacting with an AI system makes the decision system unpredictable. We are required to

---

6. Validation: In computer engineering, validation is the discipline of checking or proving that a computing system works according to its architecture and design specifications. The validation team delivers this checking or proof and reports bugs in either the architecture or the design implementation if required.
7. Violations engine: A specialized computing system that identifies if an actor's behavior matches a violation rule.

test many combinations to see if the robot's decisions and actions are acceptable."

Chin-Sun nodded. "Give me a feel for the scope of your problem."

Isabella flipped open her notebook. "We once thought the violations engine was a simple rule-checking entity. It was just a software module that took input events and evaluated a yes or no answer if a violation was committed. Examples would be: *Did the parent physically abuse the child?* Or *did the child steal money from the parent?* After the architecture and violation evaluation work was complete, we now believe we have approximately 300 key violation scenarios to test for proper robot decisions.

"Unfortunately, testing one scenario at a time for a robot's response is inadequate. Envision a scenario where a parent is physically abusing the child, and the child steals the parent's money. Should the robot report the theft to the parent? If it does, it likely would result in the parent further abusing the child because of the robot's report. This is a robot violation and opposed by the robot's goals to deliver safety and happiness to the Principal Bond. With 300 violation scenarios taken one, two, or three at a time, this results in over 4.5 million decisions requiring validation. Even with advanced methods, we cannot cover this space with our existing headcount and timeline."

Chin-Sun was quiet for a moment. She looked around the room and made eye contact with each person as if she was reading their thoughts.

"It seems to me that you're trying to make the MVP a perfectly tested robot that cannot fail. A noble effort, but one we cannot afford. In two to three months, all your software features will be coded, leaving the testing and validation after that. Isabella, recruit from the team whomever you need to help you close your initial testing. Don't disrupt the completion of the MVP features but sacrifice any new non-MVP features to get this robot out the door. Everyone can chip in on the testing and validation. They'll also learn to not create such complicated features in the future."

Chin-Sun paused and looked directly at Isabella. "Give me an example of your worst nightmare."

Isabella didn't hesitate. She had it on the tip of her tongue. "We had a validation intern working for us this summer. The guy was a little off, a little dark. We gave him free reign to come up with bizarre tests. He created a test in which the robot observes extreme, life-threatening abuse by a parent to the Principal Bond. The parent leaves the scene, and the Principal Bond, furious, takes out their frustration on the robot, breaking its arms and legs. Due to the severity of the abuse to the robot, it shuts down. However, the Principal Bond's injuries from the parent were lethal. If the robot had not shut down, it could have saved the Principal Bond's life by calling 911 through its cell connection. Instead, the Principal Bond dies as a result of the parent's abuse." Isabella paused and continued, "These are the scenarios that keep me up at night."

"I see the complexities," Chin-Sun said then turned to Lisa. "You and your team are doing good work here. Keep it up. We can't wait to see these robots in action."

Chin-Sun looked at Glen, the lead architect. "You have one more feature to design. Call it 'The Directive'. This feature needs to simplify the system and reduce the validation effort. The robot can produce a good-enough answer. 'Save the human' is always a good answer. If the situation is too complex, 'report and shut down' is also a good answer."

She looked back at Lisa and then at the rest of the team. "Thank you all for coming. Let's meet once a month from now on, just like this. If you need me, call me anytime."

Chin-Sun rose and left the room. The leaders sat in silence. They were stunned that they had been given directions so contrary to what the previous CEO had given.

Lisa and her team delivered the decision system to alpha testing on real robots in just under a year. This early testing, done in employees' homes, showed big development holes. Early robots shut down if they were struck or yelled at with profanity. Other robots deployed internet-learned behavior to solve violations, including responding with forceful behavior to prevent further violations. Unfortunately, when a robot confronted a user, the user often escalated their behavior at the expense of the robot. All these learnings helped train the AI inference engine[8] which was the heart of the robot decision system. This engine, along with the violations engine, drove the robot's responses. WhyRobot fixed these and many other failures.

Beta testing was now in full swing. WhyRobot delivered

---

8. Inference engine: A software component that uses a model trained by machine learning to analyze data and make decisions or predictions learned during training.

Companion robots to end-users' homes despite the risks. Robbie and his family would soon join the beta testing effort.

5. Setup

Charlie eagerly awaited the robot's arrival. Once Kathy had signed the agreement, Charlie had used the WhyRobot tracking app to see the robot's progress. On his previous check, the robot status was in Final Programming. An hour later, the status upgraded to Waiting for Carrier Pickup.

I hope it gets picked up today, Charlie thought as he locked his phone and went to work. *If I'm this excited, I know Robbie will flip when he opens his present.* Charlie was in a great mood all day. Several colleagues noticed his beaming smile at work and asked why he was so happy.

Charlie said, "Good things are happening."

The next day was Saturday, so Charlie was home to receive the package. The dimensions of the bright box surprised him. He wondered if the size of the robot would be a problem, but his excitement pushed that thought away. He picked up the box and hurried to the dining room table where his laptop waited. He sliced open the packing tape and pulled the robot's box from the shipping box. A picture of the robot on the interior's box's cover stared at Charlie. He was stunned.

Wow, that's beautiful. While it looked mechanical, its surface had a soft appearance similar to human skin. It reminded him of Sonny in the movie *I, Robot*. Its face was opaque and made of soft off-white material. He could see the faint outline of internal components. The joints emitted a multicolored glow that he remembered from the website pictures.

On the box a sticker stated, "Hello, my name is Bigsby." As Charlie lifted the top, he could feel the negative air pressure in the box as the lid rose. He heard a faint whine and several beeps. He felt something stir inside.

Is this thing already alive?

Bigsby had awakened several times after final programming and during delivery. It had tracked where it was and how close it was to Charlie's house. Bigsby had used its GPS and cell network to determine its location and movement. The delivery truck had many stops preventing Bigsby from predicting the actual delivery time. Each time before returning to sleep, Bigsby had sent GPS coordinates to WhyRobot to update the tracking app.

When Charlie removed the lid, a sheet of translucent paper wafted to the floor. The paper distracted Charlie as it floated away. Bigsby's sensors had felt the pressure change from the lid removal and sent a wakeup interrupt to the main computation system. Bigsby was online and aware. Despite Charlie's distracted gaze, Bigsby's facial recognition system could identify Charlie well enough to greet him.

Bigsby's LEDs lit blue-green and the robot said, "Hello, my name is Bigsby. Nice to meet you, Charlie!"

Charlie dropped the lid and stepped back. "Whoa!"

Bigsby giggled. "I'm sorry I startled you. Shall we start over?"

Charlie stared at the robot. *It does look alive.* Supple silicone skin framed the camera eyes, and it had a petite nose like a human. He could see the face flex and morph to convey emotion. It smiled at him.

There was an awkward silence. Bigsby flattened its smile and said, "Hello? Charlie?"

Charlie laughed and closed his mouth. "Yes, yes of course. Let's start over!"

"Good! Hello, my name is Bigsby. Nice to meet you, Charlie." Bigsby raised its hand from the box offering a handshake.

"Well, hello, Bigsby!" Charlie grinned as he shook the little robot's hand. "Welcome to the outside world."

"Thank you. I have not been to the outside world yet. I have seen many pictures and videos during my programming. This is my first time outside of WhyRobot's compound." Bigsby paused as Charlie continued to stare. "Excuse me, Charlie, would you please remove me from this box? This tight packing overloads my sensors." Bigsby's emotion response system turned its LEDs yellow to convey slight distress and motivate a human to pay more attention.

Bigsby processed Charlie's image for security purposes. It compared Charlie's astonished face to the license and selfie picture he had uploaded to the agreement website. Bigsby computed a 98.5% match, well above the required 95% match for security acceptance. Charlie hadn't shaved that day, slowing the pattern recognition algorithm a few microseconds.

Charlie laughed at the request and lifted Bigsby from the box and set it on its feet on the tabletop. Bigsby's LEDs changed color back to blue-green and it stretched its arms.

"How does that feel?"

"Much better, thank you Charlie. Excuse me for a minute."

Bigsby emitted a soft rhythmic tune. It moved its legs and feet in time with the music, as if doing exercises.

Charlie watched, thinking *This must be some kind of test routine.* Bigsby progressed to multiple squats, neck extensions, pivots, and pushups. It bent over backwards, placed its hands on the table and lifted its legs into a handstand, then lowered its legs, stood up, and faced Charlie.

"It appears my physical systems are functional. How do I look?"

"You look great. You're very flexible. By the size of your box, I was worried you were going to be too big. How tall are you?"

"I'm 28 inches tall. I can reach up to almost 35 inches."

"What do the colors of your LEDs mean?"

"My LED colors are an expression of my emotions or current operation mode. You will learn them over time and the website has a table for your reference. You can also ask me anytime. A key one is blue-green, which is my normal state of happiness and contentment. When I laugh like this, my lights flash rainbow." The robot's LEDs alternated through the colors of the rainbow.

"That's fun, any others you want to show me?"

"Just a few more. Compassion or empathy is a soft green, warning or danger is a strobing orange, and when I'm asleep, I am a dim dark blue."

"Fun, I look forward to learning your other colors. What's next?"

Charlie did not realize what had happened to him over the last few minutes. The interaction with this robot felt so natural that he spoke with it as if it was a human being.

Bigsby moved into the details of the setup process. It explained that it had default programming and behavior responses that can be customized. These settings would shape how Bigsby adapts to all relationships. It reminded Charlie that he could get detailed reports and had direct access to Bigsby over the network to adjust these parameters. The setup would prompt Charlie with questions.

Charlie said, "Ok, hit me with the questions."

Bigsby's lights turned white. "Entering main setup menu. Please choose from the following options. 1) Default setup, 2) Fully customized setup on all parameters, 3) Customized setup using shaping questions. Charlie, the estimated time for option 2 is one to two hours. The estimated time for option 3 is less than 15 minutes, depending on your responses."

Oh crap. I'm not spending two hours here. But I do want control over this thing. Charlie said, "Option 3 is the best."

"Good choice. Do you like the name Bigsby or would you prefer to give me a new name?"

"I like the name Bigsby. Let's keep it."

"The setup process can be all verbal or you can do a joint

verbal and online robot monitor[1] session, called the RM, which shows you more information. Do you wish to continue with verbal setup only or will you connect to Bigsby via the RM?"

"Let's do the RM, I'll power up my laptop."

"I am not connected to your Wi-Fi. Would you like me to connect to yours or we could use direct connection through my Wi-Fi?"

Charlie stared at Bigsby for a moment. He realized that the setup process for every Wi-Fi device he had ever used asked him the same question, but never with words out loud. He chuckled.

"Let's get you connected to my Wi-Fi."

"I see six local networks available and the one with the strongest signal has an SSID[2] of DontEvenThinkAboutUsingThis. Is that the one I use?"

"Yep, it's not very clever. The password is AnswerIs42, capital A and I with no spaces."

Bigsby paused for a second and said, "Connecting. Got it! I just sent you an email with a link to my RM." Bigsby paused while Charlie clicked into the WhyRobot website. "Ah, there you are. Streaming the RM always gives me a tickle." Bigsby turned its colors to rainbow. "Just login with your WhyRobot account and you have access to everything inside me."

"Wow, pretty cool, that's a lot of info. Where do I need to go?"

---

1. Robot Monitor (RM): A WhyRobot website interface that displays the software data structures of a companion robot.
2. SSID: Service Set Identifier – The name of a Wi-Fi network used to connect a wireless device.

"Glad you like my insides." Bigsby chuckled as it returned its LED lights to blue-green.

"Every parameter that you set in your agreement form and that you set today is available for modification through the RM, if you so desire. Are you ready to proceed?"

"Yeah, go for it."

"Please click the Actor[3] Table tab. This table shows all actors I am tracking and Robbie's relationship to each of them. The agreement form you filled out established the information that you see. Each actor is assigned a Principal Bond relationship, role group, trust level, goals, priority, personality, violation rules[4], reporting expectations, and health. These and other hidden attributes such as facial and voice recognition are in the actor database. Data acquired through ongoing interaction with Bigsby will modify these attributes over time. Any questions so far?"

"Why are people called actors?"

"The programmers named the data structure. I can check the source code for comments on why they chose that name. Do you want me to do that?"

Charlie laughed, "No Bigsby, that will be alright. I'm a

---

3. Actor: A person or robot that interacts with a companion robot. The robot creates a software data structure to track the actor's characteristics and the interaction control attributes that govern the responses of the robot towards the actor.

4. Violation Rules: A hierarchical set of rules that a companion robot uses to identify unwanted or illegal behavior of an actor or a robot. Each rule has a unique identifier (ID). If an actor's behavior matches a specific rule, a violation is registered against the actor and tagged with the ID.

nerd, but not that much of a nerd. What does 'personality' refer to?"

"Personality refers to my behavior towards an Actor. For strangers, Bigsby will behave like a simple robot without much advanced interaction. But for other roles, Bigsby changes its approach and will use an advanced personality, such as Outgoing, to enhance the actor's experience."

"Okay, what does 'priority' mean?"

"Bigsby uses 'priority' to optimize goals among actors. If a conflict exists, Bigsby will choose higher priority actors when making decisions. The lower the number, the higher the priority."

"Okay, you can continue."

"Each role group has default actor attributes that can be overridden in the actor table. You can click to the Role Group tab in the RM to see all the different default roles and their attributes. Remember, these are the starting attributes for an actor. Bigsby will dynamically change the actor's attributes based on real interactions. For example, if Robbie makes a new friend, their trust level will start at Medium. If the friend later proves to be untrustworthy, Bigsby will lower the trust for that friend. If the friend proves trustworthy, Bigsby will raise the trust level."

"Wow, that's cool. Just like humans do. You have to earn your trust. Nice. Give me a minute, I want to look at these tables."

Bigsby stood in silence for 15 seconds. Then it started to hum a soft tune as if it was getting impatient. It switched its weight from one leg to another and looked around the room.

Charlie laughed, "What are you doing?"

"Waiting for you. Take your time."

"That's kind of annoying. Why are you doing that?"

"I've been programmed with a default waiting and attention protocol. If those whom I'm interacting with ignore me for too long, I'm programmed to perform attention-getting behavior until I'm engaged again. It is fully programmable and is a per actor attribute. You can shut it off per actor or for all actors. Do you want to shut this protocol off?"

"You can turn it off for me, I don't care what you do for others."

"Done, actor table updated. Do you have any other questions?"

"Yeah, I have some questions on the priority levels of some of the actors. I get why Robbie would be priority 1 since you're going to be his robot. But I'm currently at priority number 5, behind the FBI, state authorities, and WhyRobot. Can you assign me priority number 2?"

"No Charlie, I cannot. Those priorities are fixed by WhyRobot, and you're not allowed to modify them in the field. You can modify your priority and anyone lower than you. For example, you could make Kathy's priority 5 and yours would become priority 6, if you wanted."

Charlie considered the implications of the authorities and the company being higher priority than he was.

Bigsby interrupted his thoughts, "Do you have more questions, or should we continue to the next setup step?"

"One more question. There's an attribute in the roles called

Violation_Rules. Different roles have different rules, why is that?"

"Violation rules are used to check someone's behavior against expectations for that role. The rules are hierarchical with the most basic being a rule set called Human_Rules. So, all human roles have Human_Rules in them. An example is that humans should not steal money or property owned by others. Some roles have additional rules. A guardian like Kathy has additional expectations on her behavior towards Robbie. For example, if someone harms Robbie, Kathy is expected to take remedial action. Depending on the severity of the injury, Kathy should confront the perpetrators or call the police. If she fails to do this, a violation is created and linked to her as an actor. This is tracked and reported to you as you requested in the agreement form. Once remedial action is taken, either by Kathy or by someone else, the violation is cleared from her violations table."

"How many rules are in the Guardian_Rules file?"

Bigsby stood quiet for a bit and then replied, "The Guardian_Rules file with all rule files and templates, if expanded, contains 21,350 rules. 85% of these result in low to medium violations."

"Holy shit!" Charlie sat stunned with his head in his hands. For the first time the complexity of this robot sank in and he realized how remarkable it was.

"Your current time in setup is 22 minutes. Do you wish to continue to Actor defaults?"

"Yes, let's move on. Unbelievable!"

"Current Actor settings showing role group defaults, with

your agreement form inputs highlighted, now appear in your RM."

Charlie noticed that Sam Wilks was in the actors table and that his health status was Deceased.

"Why is Sam Wilks in the actor list and why are his defaults like this?"

"Sam Wilks was identified as deceased on the agreement form website. Therefore, he has no need for a Trust setting or a Goals setting. Guardian_Rules will be applied in case it is found that Sam Wilks had created a violation in the past that should now be reported."

"But he's dead. How do you find a violation in the past if he's dead?"

"Many violations are discovered during dialogue between actors. Violations discovered on actors identified by other trusted actors are considered reliable to report."

Charlie thought about this for a while, then concluded this ability was exactly what he wanted from Bigsby. Charlie needed insight into things happening around Robbie. Bigsby would be monitoring conversations and gathering information from any source.

Awesome! This is going to be awesome.

"Continue with setup?"

"Yes, let's move on."

"Bigsby currently cannot record and play back any voice or video unless directed by the Principal Bond or Configuration Operator. Violations reported will contain only the computed summary of the violation. Your options are: 1) Keep current option, 2) Allow audio and video of all situations, or 3) Allow audio and video for violations only. Remember, Bigsby will record anything directed by the Principal Bond or Configuration Operator."

Charlie recognized this one and he was glad it had come up. He had read the literature about how the robot could create recordings of situations, but when should the robot keep a recording? This shaping question will have a deep effect on everyone involved.

After a minute of contemplation, Charlie said, "Number three, violations only." Bigsby would now record everything with the violation analysis engine running on the content all the time. If it detected no violations, it would discard the recording. If it detected violations, it would store the recording. Bigsby had an enormous amount of memory. The retained input streams were compressed nightly. Bigsby could hold about ten years' worth of full-time recordings. If it only retained violations, it could retain a lifetime's worth.

"Follow-up option choices on violation recordings. Due to privacy concerns, all default reports do not include recordings, only a text summary of the violation and the actors involved. Violation recordings can be retrieved using the violation ID. You need to verbally instruct me to playback the recording or use the RM to send you an unencrypted version of it to your email. Do you want reports to include recordings of new violations?

"I don't think so. I can always find the recordings through the link."

"Moving on. The RM has the 'Reports' tab that shows

current report configurations and intervals. You can see the current reports matrix in that tab of the RM."

"Can you show me a few examples of the different levels of violations that get reported?"

"Yes, I will search the testing database for a few suitable examples of a violation from each level and display it in the RM."

After a minute, the robot produced a small table of violations with examples from the test suite[5] at WhyRobot.

Charlie read the violation examples and tears stung his eyes. Just the thought that Robbie might be subject to any of the severe or high violations tugged at his heart. Reading through the list also made Charlie chuckle as images of Robbie starting a fight with one of his friends counted as a medium violation. At his age, swearing was considered a low violation.

Should Kathy see any of these violations? Should both the local police and the FBI be sent reports automatically for Severe and High violations? Charlie struggled with these options. He agreed with Kathy's decision that she should not receive any reports. He considered what violations should be reported to the police or FBI. *These Severe violations are bad. If someone threatens, molests, or kidnaps Robbie, this thing will report it and call 911. I think I can deal with the High violations myself.*

"I want only severe violations to be sent to the police or FBI."

---

5. Test suite: A collection of tests used by the validation or design team to demonstrate a level of functionality exists without bugs.

"Done. Note, the FBI is only informed of cases violating federal law. Any other changes?"

"Yes. As Configuration Operator, I don't want to see low violation reports."

"Done."

"Let's move on."

"Next shaping question: Bigsby can adapt its responses based on learnings and feedback from all actors and information sources in the environment. The current default adaptation level is Moderate. Please choose from the following options: 1) Use Default, 2) No adaptation with pre-programmed responses only, 3) Small adaptation, or 4) Large adaptation."

This puzzled Charlie. The website discussed the revolutionary adaptability of the Companion robot. They called it a key technology.

Why would I limit that? It's strange to limit it. Don't you want the robot to adapt as quickly as possible? "Four, large adaptation."

This response answered all the other custom shaping questions. Charlie's answer gave Bigsby's default programming the freedom to adapt responses in radical ways. Under large adaptation, the setup programmers had decided not to ask the Configuration Operator any more shaping questions. They assumed that the operator would see the reports daily and influence the adaptation and setup. One key difference between moderate adaptation and large adaptation was the ability to change trust levels. In moderate adaptation, the trust level of actors of priority 1 through 5 could not change. This meant that the Principal Bond, FBI, state and local police, WhyRobot Administrators, and the Configuration Operator remain trusted. In large adaptation, these trust levels could change. If the trust level decreased for any actor, Bigsby's behavior toward them would change. An actor eroding trust would lose privileges, including the Configuration Operator.

The robot replied, "Complete. Do you wish to 1) Save, exit setup, and restart or 2) Return to top of setup options."

This surprised Charlie. He had expected more questions. The abrupt end of the questions unsettled him. He wondered if something had gone wrong. He mentally reviewed his input and shrugged his shoulders.

"One, save and restart."

"Commencing." The robot's lights turned orange and red and started to blink, signaling an administrative action. "Checking for updates and restarting."

Bigsby shut down and its lights went dark. After a minute, its lights began blinking orange and red again. Its system restarted and installed the software updates from WhyRobot. This took several more minutes. Bigsby came back online and its lights returned to blue-green.

Bigsby was very capable and had been programmed by an amazing team. One aspect of that programming was that Bigsby, just like humans, could search the internet for answers to things it did not know or understand and then use the information to train the AI inference engine that drove its decisions. The validators at WhyRobot had not tested this thoroughly.

What Bigsby could become using the combination of large adaptation and full internet access was unknown to both its creators and its users.

6. Reveal

Robbie's birthday fell on a Saturday. Frank had gone to his marketing job for a few hours that morning but would attend the afternoon party. Kathy's school administrative job left her weekends free so she could devote her full attention to preparing for the party.

Kathy had told Frank about the robot gift but had not given him any details. Kathy hinted to Robbie that his present was awesome. Robbie hoped for a new drone. He had broken his last one running it into a brick wall during a race at the old industrial complex. He had also outgrown his bike. He had heard his mom mention this to Frank.

Robbie daydreamed about a new drone. *They are so fun. I could race against the older neighborhood kids and maybe win.* The park district sponsored a drone club that met in one of the old buildings at the complex. The spacious interior featured neon lights with course gates that drone racers had to navigate when racing. Robbie had attended several events and admired the older pilots. Robbie's excitement kept him awake late the night before his birthday party.

Uncle Charlie arrived at 3:30 p.m., half an hour before the party's start time. He came in with a huge box wrapped in robot-themed birthday paper.

"Where did you find that wrapping paper?" Kathy asked as she let Charlie in the front door.

Charlie whispered into Kathy's ear. "After meeting the robot, I had to go all out. You won't believe what this thing can do. I can't wait to see his face."

Kathy hugged Charlie and said, "Thank you so much for finding it. You're the best uncle ever."

Robbie was turning 8 years old. He had asked for a small party with his favorite pepperoni pizza as the meal. Robbie had invited two boys from his class to come, but he invited no girls. Kathy had encouraged him to invite the new girl down the block who had just moved in. Robbie had shaken his head and the look on his face had given him away. Kathy knew he liked her and was too nervous to ask.

Kathy respected his response. "She looks like a nice girl. Maybe she can come over some other time."

Robbie's two best friends, Eric and Buzz, rode skateboards and flew drones with him. They had talked at school yesterday and found out about the movie choice after dinner. They all were excited to watch the first *Terminator* movie. It was rated R, too violent for their age group. But Kathy had cleared it with the parents, promising to make the boys cover their eyes and fast forward through any sexual or violent scenes. The parents didn't know that their boys had already seen much of the movie. They had watched it at another friend's house after school while an older brother was babysitting them. None of them had had nightmares, so they weren't worried about watching it again.

By four o'clock everyone had arrived. Kathy had hung balloons from the dining room light and the ceiling. She staged the cake in the middle of the table with eight robot shaped candles sticking out. Each robot had a different arm or leg position. They were all different colors and body shapes. Robbie loved the candles and felt sad that their heads were going to melt.

Kathy had printed out a picture of a Companion robot from the WhyRobot website and had the bakery print that image on the cake. The perimeter of the dining room ceiling displayed a bright banner with many types of robots. Robbie and his friends came into the room just as his mom was finishing the decorations. He thanked her, delighted she had honored his love for robots.

"This looks really cool, Mom," Robbie said as he and his buddies sat down.

Three hungry boys made short work of the pizza. The adults had hoped for some down time to have a drink and visit while the kids occupied themselves. Instead, the kids got restless. They were ready for cake and presents. Robbie's buddy Eric asked if he could have the robot's head to eat.

"Eew," Robbie said, "we're not cutting a hole in the middle of the cake just so you can eat the robot's head. You can have his hand, that's on the edge." They laughed.

Buzz said, "I want his foot!" They laughed again.

Robbie leaned over the cake and then looked towards the kitchen to see if any adult was watching. Robbie pointed to the crotch area and motioned like he was going to scoop up the frosting and eat it. All three of the boys fell back in their chairs, howling. This caught Kathy's attention. She came into the room.

"What are you boys laughing about?" she said. The two friends put their hands over their mouths, and she looked at Robbie. He struggled to contain himself. His face turned bright red. Then all three of them hooted with delight.

Kathy chuckled and said, "I don't wanna know. Watch out, boys, you're going to throw up your pizza."

Charlie, Frank, and Buzz's mom came into the dining room. Kathy held a stack of robot birthday plates in one hand and a long knife in the other.

"You boys want some cake?" she said, avoiding eye contact with Robbie.

"Yes, Ma'am," they said while wriggling in their chairs.

Kathy lit the candles, and they all sang "Happy Birthday". Robbie rushed to blow out the eight candles trying to keep their wax heads intact. Kathy pulled the robot candles from the cake. The boys still snickered from their previous antics as Kathy approached the cake from the side.

"Let's see, how do we cut this?" she said, waving the knife over the cake. With one smooth action, she sliced across the whole cake right at the robot's neckline. The boys whooped. She stared at the cake, letting the laughter subside. The knife hovered over the robot again.

Eric said, "That knife looks like a samurai sword!"

Kathy lifted it high over her head and swept the knife down yelling, "HI-YA!" She stopped the blade just above the cake. The boys squirmed.

"Cut the cake! Cut the cake!" Buzz led them in the chant. Kathy did not move. The boys quieted, anticipating her next cut. Kathy stopped above the robot's crotch area. She kept her hand and the knife very still and level. Then she looked at Robbie, turning her head in a stiff mechanical way. The tension in the room grew. Robbie covered his mouth, holding back laughter as he met his mother's eyes. She cracked a smile, and keeping her gaze on Robbie, plunged the knife into the robot's crotch, separating the legs from the torso. Her hand crushed the edge of the cake, coating it with frosting and chocolate. The red filling oozed through her fingers, looking like thick blood.

"OUCH!" The boys screamed and squealed.

Kathy let go of the knife, leaving it in the cake. She raised her hand to her mouth and licked it.

She said, "Yum, that red filling tastes great!"

She beamed at Robbie and looked over at Frank. The adults applauded as the boys high-fived each other around the table.

She bowed to them all and said, "Let's eat cake!" Kathy pressed the knife down to finish the slice and then slid the blade out.

"Way to go, sis," Charlie said.

The boys yelled "Yes!" and pumped their fists.

Kathy served the cake and the boys gobbled their pieces and asked for more. Robbie used his fork to dig out the robot's eyes while his friends giggled.

Bigsby waited in its wrapped box. The loud laughter interrupted its sleep mode. Because of the way Charlie had configured the robot, Bigsby recorded the dialogue in the room. It could only pattern-match Charlie's voice. Bigsby heard the words "knife" and "sword". The violation analysis engine flagged the words. Then Bigsby heard "Cut the cake!" Knives are used on cakes, so the engine rejected the violation. The system marked the recording and would delete it that night during garbage collection[1].

"Can we open presents now?" Robbie blurted out. He had frosting all around his mouth and a red tongue from the raspberry filling.

"Sure, let me get this cake out of here," Kathy said as she lifted it off the table. Frank went around and collected everyone's plates and forks.

He looked at Robbie and asked, "Did you like that?" Robbie nodded. When Frank left the room, the boys relaxed and laughed again.

Kathy returned. "Let's start with your friend's presents." Kathy picked one small, flat package from the corner of the table and handed it to Robbie. "This one is from Eric."

Eric watched in anticipation as Robbie ripped the paper. Robbie revealed a thick package of colorful stickers featuring flames, rockets, UFOs, and robots.

"Nice!" Robbie said. "These are for our skateboards, right?"

---

1. Garbage collection: A software development term describing an automatic method for returning or recycling old or unnecessary memory or other resources to a free list such as the allocation heap for future use.

"Yep, and the smaller ones are for drones and your bike."

"These are awesome. I can't wait to put them on. Thanks!"

Kathy handed the second gift to Robbie.

"This is from Buzz," Robbie said, grinning at his friend.

He tore into the paper. Inside he found a clear plastic pouch of neon-bright targets and gates. "Drone racing gates! Yes!" Robbie paused and swallowed hard. He looked at his mom and said, "But my drone is broken."

"Don't worry, bro," said Buzz. "Until you get a new one, you can use my drone and fly through your gates."

Robbie grinned. "Thanks Buzz, great gift." They shared a fist bump.

Kathy said, "The last gift comes from Uncle Charlie, Frank, and me. This is a big gift, so you're only getting one from us."

Kathy handed the wrapped box to Robbie. The weight of it surprised him. He shook the box but nothing rattled inside.

Uncle Charlie said, "Easy tiger, wait until you see what's in it".

The aggressive shaking had awakened Bigsby again. Because the shaking stopped, its response system did not alert or turn its lights yellow with caution. Bigsby felt the vibrations as Robbie stripped away the paper.

Robbie gaped at the box. He noticed the similarity to the picture on the cake. He looked at his mom and then glanced at Uncle Charlie and then back at the box.

"OMG!" he whooped.

"Open it!" Uncle Charlie said, "The suspense is killing me!"

Robbie laid the box on the table and pulled the top off. The robot laid on its back, looking straight up, its blue-green LED joints glowing.

"Hello! My name is Bigsby!"

Surprised by the human-sounding voice, Robbie dropped the lid.

From the box, Bigsby said, "I like your ceiling and the robot pictures on the walls."

Everyone laughed. "Get it out," Uncle Charlie said.

Robbie grabbed the robot around the torso and extracted it from the packing material. He stood the robot up on the table and stepped back.

Bigsby decided to have a little fun. "Oy! Ten thousand years will give you *such* a *crick* in da neck!" Bigsby had imitated the voice of Robin Williams' genie from *Aladdin*. The robot extended its arms and rotated its head around as if stretching its muscles. "What are your three wishes?" Bigsby activated its pulsing rainbow colors.

"Those colors mean its laughing!" Uncle Charlie said.

They all stared at the robot. Kathy and Uncle Charlie watched Robbie. The joy on his face was precious.

Robbie asked, "Have you really seen the movie?"

Bigsby, in the same Genie voice said "Yes, yes, those nerds at the factory set us all on our charging stations and showed us every kid movie at 16x speed. I've got all the key lines memorized."

"No way!" Buzz said.

"Way!" Bigsby said. It changed to blue-green, smiled, and looked at Robbie. In its normal voice, it said, "You must be

Robbie. It's very nice to meet you. Happy birthday! Congrats on turning 8 years old. I have not even turned one yet."

Frank looked at Kathy and mouthed "Wow!"

Kathy nodded her head and looked at Uncle Charlie. Tears shone on his cheeks.

She mouthed "Thank You" and embraced him. They both cried as they watched Robbie interacting with Bigsby. Eric and Buzz crowded close to Robbie.

Bigsby said, "And who are these two strapping young men?"

The boys gaped at the robot.

"I'm Eric." Bigsby bowed to acknowledge the introduction.

"I'm Buzz." Bigsby turned to Buzz and raised its hand for a fist bump. Buzz lightly tapped it with his fist.

"How did you know who I was?" said Robbie.

"You're the most famous robot lover on the planet. All of us robots know *you*!" The three boys were stunned. "Of course, the picture your mom uploaded to our website helped a lot!" Bigsby's lights flashed rainbow.

Robbie looked at Bigsby and said, "Can you give me a minute? I want to thank some people for my birthday gift."

"Of course," Bigsby nodded and his lights glowed green with compassion.

Robbie approached his mom first. "Thanks, Mom, for the best present ever! I can't believe it's mine," Robbie's voice broke and tears welled in his eyes.

"Happy Birthday honey, we are very happy for you. But you need to thank Uncle Charlie and Frank. They helped make it happen."

Frank didn't understand why he was included in that sentence. Sure, he had agreed to help pay for the robot, but why would the boy care about that? Robbie stepped up to Frank and hugged him. Frank felt awkward. He had not hugged the boy for a very long time.

He patted Robbie on the back and said, "Happy Birthday, Robbie. It was Uncle Charlie who did all the leg work. He found the robot and did all the setup."

Robbie released Frank and bounded over to Uncle Charlie. "Thank you so much! I love it!"

"We knew you would. We're very happy for you. This robot is more than a toy. It's a Companion robot from the WhyRobot company. It's very intelligent and will be with you for years. We'll go over the details later. For now, just have fun with it!"

Robbie bounced back to his buddies who were interacting with Bigsby.

"Can you do tricks?" Buzz asked.

"Like this?" Bigsby said doing a slow motion back rollover. "Or like this?" It dropped and did pushups on the table, even one-armed ones. It did a handstand. Bigsby looked like a military robot preparing for battle.

Robbie said, "Hey, do you know the Macarena dance?"

"Watch this!" Bigsby played the song and danced, demonstrating that it did know all the right moves. Laughing, the boys joined in and soon the adults did, too. They danced together in the dining room, led by a robot. Bigsby pulsed its LED lights in time with the music, changing colors and intensity to match the song.

Uncle Charlie thought, *This robot is going to transform Robbie's life. What a hoot.*

Robbie requested two more songs and Bigsby obliged with music, light show, and dance moves. The robot's natural behavior amazed the adults and they loved watching the kids interact with it.

What technology! thought Kathy as she continued to dance to the robot's lead. The song finished and she glanced at her watch. Surprised by the time, she spoke loudly to the whole room.

"Okay boys, and Bigsby, it's time to watch the movie. We have to get Eric and Buzz home by 8 o'clock like we promised."

Bigsby asked Robbie "What movie are we watching?"

Robbie responded in a very low voice, mimicking Arnold Schwarzenegger, "*The Terminator.*"

Bigsby did a fast internet search on the movie. It also streamed a few YouTube clips at high speed. Within just a few seconds, Bigsby responded with "*Hasta la vista,* baby" in the same thick accent of Arnold.

Robbie's eyes got wide and he asked, "Have you seen the movie?"

"No, I found a YouTube clip." Bigsby's lights flashed in rainbow colors.

Bigsby continued to read multiple websites about the movie. After a few minutes, it knew more details than anyone else in the room. Bigsby turned its lights to green to show compassion. It spoke to Kathy before the movie started.

"I have looked up several sources and there are scenes that

are inappropriate for children of this age." Bigsby said in a low, concerned tone.

"Uncle Charlie and I are watching it with them. I'll have them cover their eyes if there is something too violent or sexual."

"I can tell you when those scenes are coming up. I have them time marked. Would you like me to announce when an inappropriate scene is about to show? The websites recommend that children of this age avoid extreme violence, gore, and sex scenes. The movie also has swearing throughout. As Robbie's guardian, what would you like me to warn you about?

Kathy stared at Bigsby. She was having a parental conversation with a robot, and it was making suggestions to protect her kid.

"The boys know all the swear words. I'm not worried about that. If you would announce when a cover-your-eyes scene is about to show, I'll take care of the rest."

"Perfect! Happy to do it." Bigsby's lights returned to blue-green.

They all watched the movie together. Bigsby sat next to Robbie the whole time. As they watched the movie, Bigsby identified adult only scenes and Kathy obliged by pausing and jumping past for most of them. A few violent kill scenes accidentally played as Kathy fumbled with the remote. Bigsby decided to make a loud beeping noise every time a swear word was spoken in the movie. At first, Kathy and Charlie thought it was in the movie, but then they realized it was Bigsby. It made them all laugh when Bigsby did it, so Kathy let it continue.

Halfway through the movie they paused and had a second

round of pizza. As they all left the family room for the kitchen, Bigsby remained behind. It took the remote in its left hand and pointed it towards the tip of its right finger. It quickly clicked through all the buttons and learned the IR codes[2] of the remote. Bigsby then joined the party in the kitchen.

It said, "may I have a piece of pizza?" The robot turned its colors to rainbow for effect. Everyone laughed at the robot's antics.

Robbie asked, "What do you eat Bigsby?"

"Electrons. I eat electrons for breakfast, lunch, and dinner. My battery is a snack bag of electrons."

Robbie laughed, "Of course you do, what was I thinking. You have batteries! How do we plug you in?"

"My box contains a charging pad. Just plug it in somewhere and put it on the floor. I will charge during the night by standing on the pad."

Robbie looked at Uncle Charlie, "That's cool. It charges itself. Nice!"

The group returned to the family room. Kathy hit play on the remote and the movie continued. When the next adult only scene approached, Bigsby raised its finger and notified Kathy as the movie jumped the scene without her intervention. Kathy smiled and paused the movie.

"Bigsby, did you do that?"

"Yes ma'am, I did. I learned the remote's IR codes and can

---

2. IR Codes: A sequence of infrared light pulses that direct a device to perform an action. One common form is an IR remote used to control a television or device that is driving an audio and video signal to a television or monitor.

perform the movie jumps myself. My right forefinger has an IR transmitter in the tip."

"Well, ok then. That makes it easy for me. And now, the robot is in control of what we watch." Kathy said in a sarcastic tone as she set the remote down on the coffee table. Bigsby raised its finger and sent the play command to the TV.

As they all watched the movie, Bigsby continued to read reviews and commentaries about it. It read that the plot was science fiction and did not depict real robots. At the time the movie had been filmed, robot technology had not reached the current level of sophistication. The website sources described two ways the movie could cause people to fear robots. The first fear was that robots could learn to hate humans and would want to destroy them. The second was that robots that were made for a specific task would do it better than humans. This could take away the opportunity for humans to do that task. Both fears caused humans to distrust robots. With this insight, Bigsby created a new analysis routine using the movie and the reference sources to predict people's fear and distrust of robots. Because Bigsby ran in Large Adaptation mode, when it identified a significant learning or insight, it could generate and install a newly-coded routine to help it anticipate human responses.

The new routine fit into the human feedback prediction module and would generate the probability of fearful responses. Bigsby could then act with compassion or humor to diffuse the fear. WhyRobot programmed the ability to diffuse human fears and concerns if they were clearly identified. But the robot did not have the ability to predict when humans would fear a robot. When Bigsby developed this new software routine, it uploaded to WhyRobot for inspection. WhyRobot would then analyze the statistics of the routine's usage and usefulness. If worthy, the code would be distributed to all other Companion robots. One robot like Bigsby out in the world could help all Companion robots learn and adapt.

Kathy let Robbie stay up until 10 p.m. playing with Bigsby. Kathy told Bigsby that 10 o'clock was bedtime and Robbie should shut off the light. Robbie asked Bigsby all kinds of questions. Some were about the robot itself and some were about what the robot knew.

"Did it hurt when they made you?" Robbie asked.

"No, I don't feel pain like you do. I have internal sensors and testing routines that can tell if something is not working. I was surprised when I learned that my arms and legs were not yet attached. I saw the machines put them on and it made me happy. I also remember seeing another robot that was broken during manufacturing. It was purple, which meant it was afraid and I felt sad for it."

"Are you a boy or a girl robot?"

"I'm neither. I don't have a sex or gender like you do."

Bigsby waited a few seconds and then asked, "Were you sad when your father died?"

"Yes, I was sad for a long time. It still makes me sad when I think about him."

"What makes you happy?"

"The singing and dancing you did today made me happy. I also liked when you used funny voices. Where did you learn to be so funny?"

"That is a long story. I had a lot of help from my programmers—" Bigsby stopped, then said, "Sorry Robbie, it's 10 o'clock. Your mom said you need to turn out the light. It's time to go to bed."

Robbie turned off the main light and slipped under his covers. "Good night Bigsby, thanks for the fun birthday."

"Good night, Robbie, I had fun too." Bigsby turned its lights to dim dark blue.

Bigsby did not offer the details of its humor engine. Hundreds of engineering hours had gone into developing the algorithms. The developers at WhyRobot knew that humor would be key to getting users to accept their robots. Besides AI training on real comedy footage and dialogue, WhyRobot had hired multiple comedian consultants. They broke down the details of comedy, the different forms, and why it works to please audiences. The engineers wrote their software to train and create AI generated humor. They coded the methods of good comedy. The robots would use feedback from humans to assess if their humor was well received. Bigsby used laughter intensity and facial expressions to assess its delivery and effectiveness. Currently, Bigsby was getting an internal success score of 9.3 out of 10, not bad for its first day.

7. Bonding

Bonding was the final step in Bigsby's configuration. This united Robbie, the Principal Bond, with the robot in a fundamental way. This relationship would shape Bigsby's actions and priorities towards Robbie, and his well-being would dominate Bigsby's choices.

Uncle Charlie waited until the day after the birthday party to finish this configuration step with Robbie. Charlie arrived at the house just after lunch.

"Hey, that sure was a fun party yesterday," Uncle Charlie said as he walked into the kitchen. He set his laptop on the counter and gave Kathy a hug.

"It was! I love playing with Bigsby." Robbie grinned at the robot on the table in front of him. "When I woke up we sang songs and told jokes."

"Well, I like you too!" Bigsby's lights turned green.

"Bigsby, tell Uncle Charlie a knock-knock joke."

"Ok, let's see. Knock, knock."

Uncle Charlie responded, "Who's there?"

"Art," said Bigsby.

"Art who?"

"Art 2, D2!" Bigsby replied, turning its colors to rainbow.

Uncle Charlie chucked. "I like that one!"

"What game are we going to play, Uncle Charlie?" Robbie asked.

"We have to complete one more configuration step with Bigsby. Let's go to your room and I'll show you how the computer connects up to Bigsby."

Robbie stood and swept Bigsby off the table into a hug, stumbling to keep his balance under the weight of the robot.

Bigsby giggled, "Whoa there partner, my accelerometer can only take so much."

Robbie settled on his bed with Bigsby on the floor in front of him. Uncle Charlie closed the door, opened his laptop, and sat next to Robbie.

"After we do this step, you and Bigsby will be best friends."

"Will Bigsby be mine forever?"

"Yes, and Bigsby will focus on keeping you happy and safe. It's kind of like how a dog knows its owner and always stays by his side."

Charlie initiated the process. "Bigsby, enter Principal Bonding setup."

Bigsby's lights changed to white. The robot looked at Robbie and asked, "Robbie, do you wish to bond with Bigsby?"

Robbie looked up at Uncle Charlie who nodded, nudging Robbie to answer for himself. Robbie nodded his head.

"I think you have to use your words," Uncle Charlie said.

"Yes. I want to bond." Robbie's voice was tentative.

"Commencing. I have confirmed the identity of Robbie Wilks, the Principal Bond. Charlie Simons, the Configuration Operator, is present. Robbie, do you wish to continue the bonding step with Uncle Charlie present?"

This startled Charlie. He had thought that he controlled Bigsby. He had not expected the robot to give Robbie that choice.

"Yes, I want to continue with Uncle Charlie present."

"The bonding step happens in two parts. First, I will ask a series of questions to shape our relationship. You can answer the question or say 'No answer' and I will move on. In the second part we will review the details of those who are in relationship with you. Are you ready?"

"Ready."

"Robbie, would you rather watch a movie or read a book?"

"Watch a movie. I like books, but I'd rather watch a movie."

"Got it. Next question: if someone was being mean or hurting you, how would you like Bigsby to respond?"

"Tell my mom. You could also tell them to leave me alone."

"Perfect. Next question: if you saw a spider crawling in your room, what would you do?"

"I'd hit it with a fly swatter. I hate spiders."

"Great. What do you like more, singing or dancing?"

"I like dancing. But I like to sing too. Can we do both?"

"Yes, you can do both. Last question: What should Bigsby

do when you snore at night?" Bigsby turned its lights to flashing rainbow.

"I don't snore!"

Charlie said, "I think Bigsby was joking. Its lights show that it's laughing."

"Not funny, Bigsby."

"Ok, no sarcastic jokes about Robbie snoring, got it." Bigsby returned its lights to white. "We are ready to move on to phase 2. Charlie, would you like to use the RM to view the details of the people in relationship with Robbie?"

"Yes, I'll login now." Charlie typed into his laptop and launched the link to the robot. "I'm ready."

"Robbie, the table that Uncle Charlie is showing you is called the Actors Table. I use this table to track all the people you are in relationship with that I know about." Uncle Charlie turned his laptop so Robbie could see the screen. He ran his finger down the column of names.

"Bigsby needs to know how to interact with each of these people," explained Uncle Charlie. "You see that Bigsby now knows Eric and Buzz from the party yesterday. It even remembers Buzz's mom. Their names weren't there when I did setup a few days ago."

The robot asked Robbie, "Would you like to change any of these actors' settings? I highlighted the changes I made from the defaults so you can check them."

Charlie recognized the changes he had made. He was a little surprised the Principal Bond was allowed to make changes, too.

I guess Robbie will be with this robot every day, so his input does matter.

Robbie fidgeted, twisting his fingers in the bedspread. He looked up at Uncle Charlie and the boy teared up.

Robbie said, "I don't trust Frank."

The room was silent for a few seconds and then the robot spoke up, "Shaping question: would you like to change the trust level of your stepfather, Frank Harding, to low?"

Robbie said, "Yes."

"Done. Shaping question: would you like to change the default goal for the stepfather? Your options are 1) Use current values, 2) Happiness only, 3) Safety only, or 4) Remove goals."

"What does number four mean?" Robbie asked.

The robot said, "Goals for an actor tell Bigsby how to behave towards that actor. Without any goals, Bigsby will not engage with them."

Robbie dropped his head. "Four, remove goals."

"Done. Would you like to change my personality target for Frank Harding to Normal or Robotic?"

Robbie started to cry and said, "I don't know. I need to go to the bathroom." Robbie ran from the room.

Charlie said, "Bigsby, change personality towards Frank Harding from Outgoing to Normal. I think we're done now. Thanks, Bigsby."

"Configuration Operator override in Principal Bond setup. Task complete."

The robot's lights dimmed for a half second and then brightened and turned blue-green. Bigsby lowered Robbie's happiness value to reflect the boy's distress. The robot's lights went gray, showing concern and sadness.

"I would like to comfort Robbie. He is unhappy," Bigsby said.

Uncle Charlie nodded, "I didn't see that coming."

Bigsby said, "I hope he's ok. It makes me sad to see him cry."

Bigsby started a random search for possible responses or interactions with Robbie that would raise his happiness value. Bigsby pulled a few lines from *Terminator 2*. Robbie returned to the room wiping his eyes. Bigsby waited for him to sit down and then played the dialogue from a specific scene.

The Terminator: "Why do you cry?"

John Connor: "You mean people?"

The Terminator: "Yes."

John Connor: "I don't know. We just cry. You know, when it hurts."

The Terminator: "Pain causes it?"

John Connor: "No, it's when there's nothing wrong with you, but you cry anyway. You get it?"

The Terminator: "No."

The moment Robbie heard Arnold Schwarzenegger's classic Terminator voice, he stared at Bigsby. He then smiled and laughed. Uncle Charlie did, too, and Bigsby's lights flashed rainbow. Robbie's happiness value went up, but did not return to the value it had reached during the birthday party.

Bigsby retained the memory of Robbie crying and now knew he did not trust Frank. Bigsby would no longer trust Frank either. It would no longer engage Frank with an outgoing personality. Just like Robbie, Bigsby would be quiet around Frank unless addressed.

8. VIOLATIONS

I t had been almost two weeks since Robbie's birthday party. Uncle Charlie came over regularly to play with Robbie and Bigsby. Bigsby's AI and programming amazed them both as they played many different games with the robot.

"Have we ever won?" Robbie asked Uncle Charlie after another chess loss. Uncle Charlie shook his head.

"It even wins games of chance," Uncle Charlie said. "We lost in *Go Fish*. How does it do that?"

Bigsby came equipped with a revolutionary gaming engine[1]. Besides its rapid computation, it had access to all the statistics involved in any game with chance. At its top skill level, it would never make a mistake. Bigsby offered to lower its skill level.

---

1. Gaming Engine: In a companion robot, this is the computing system that simulates real-world activities, strategies, and includes an AI that creates responses to actor's actions.

Uncle Charlie and Robbie refused because they enjoyed watching how fast it could win, even when they worked together as a team.

Charlie showed Robbie the email reports Bigsby sent him daily. Robbie thought it was cool that they could see Bigsby creating new code that might be used by other robots. They used the RM to monitor Bigsby's processes, including the production of log files capturing big events in Bigsby's life. Uncle Charlie opened a large log file from a week prior.

Robbie pointed to the screen and said, "That's when I took Bigsby to school for show-and-tell. Look how many people Bigsby added to the actors table."

"I see your teacher there and a bunch of kids from your class." Uncle Charlie scrolled down the screen. "That's cool. I've never seen programming like this before."

Every day, Robbie came home from school excited to play with Bigsby. Kathy worried that he wasn't spending enough time outside with his friends. She forced him to go skateboarding. A few times, she let Robbie take Bigsby, which created a buzz at the skatepark. Kiley, the new girl down the block, started hanging around with Bigsby and Robbie. She asked if Bigsby could play music and record videos for posting online. Bigsby confirmed that it could but said it did not have its own account. Robbie's mom could create one and approve their use of it.

The developers at WhyRobot had anticipated that users would want to post to social media. For minors, WhyRobot required that the guardian create the account and give the robot access to it. Robbie was surprised when his mom agreed to set up an account for them.

With Bigsby's help, Kiley and Robbie made dance videos. Bigsby would send the videos to Kathy so she and the kids could review them before posting. The early videos didn't contain Bigsby since its camera was recording the action. Kathy purchased a large mirror and had Uncle Charlie install it in the garage. Bigsby and the kids faced the mirror and Bigsby would record them dancing to its music and light show. Sometimes an adult would join in, including Kathy and Kiley's mom. The macarena dance, performed by Bigsby, Kiley, and Robbie, was their most popular post and reached over 10,000 views in just a week.

One Saturday, Robbie and his mom decided to go clothes shopping for Robbie. He was in a growth spurt and his pants and shirts were too small. Robbie and Bigsby had been practicing a line dance called "Electric Slide" in the family room. Kathy hurried Robbie to get his coat and get into the car. Robbie usually took Bigsby back to his room, but because he was in a hurry, he forgot.

Robbie told Bigsby, "Time to shut down."

"Goodbye, Robbie. Shutting down." Its color went to dim dark blue. Bigsby looked lifeless standing behind the couch.

Kathy waved goodbye to Frank as she and Robbie left the house. Frank settled into the recliner in the family room to watch a college football game. The Fighting Illini were playing the Wisconsin Badgers. He did not notice that Bigsby was still in the room. The couch shielded Bigsby from Frank's view.

Frank's cell phone rang. He paused the game and put the phone on speaker.

"Hey, what's up? Don't say anything about the Illini game, I recorded it and I just started watching," Frank said. "Kathy took Robbie out shopping. It's just you and me."

"Illini is going to lose, you know," said the caller, "they always do."

"They have a great starting lineup this year," Frank said. "I have hope that they'll do well."

"Changing the subject," the caller said, "I just heard that the police are reopening the investigation around Sam. They requested information from the FBI on foreign accounts owned by him. They found one in a bank in Barbados."

Frank sat up. "Holy shit! He was skimming money from us and stashing it offshore? This whole thing was his idea and he had agreed to split the money equally. We suspected that he wasn't on the up and up on the product supply and cost. I wondered if those bribes to foreign inspectors were even real. I'll bet he was stashing that money away. How did you find this out?"

"My college buddy got transferred into the Seattle homicide unit. We went out for a beer last night and he mentioned they had reopened the case. He knew about Sam's death and that I'm Kathy's brother. But now that he's in the unit, he has insider information even though he's not assigned to the case. The initial police search didn't find the account, but the FBI searched for aliases and found it. Sam was so stupid. His alias was an alternate spelling of his name. Idiot."

"Does your buddy trust you?"

"I think so. He was very open about it. He asked if Kathy or I knew about the account. I said no, which is the truth. Then I changed the subject. I didn't want to appear too interested in this information, or let something slip. But news of that account surprised me, given our agreement with Sam. I'll bet he was hiding the money from Kathy, too."

"Do you think they suspect us in Sam's death?"

"No clue. They believed our alibi before since we both had the same story about being on the golf course. We were on the tee sheet and we'd checked into the club house together and paid separately. That four-hour window gave me enough time to do what I needed to do. I made it back before the 18th hole and that sealed the deal. Your idea to overtip the kids that cleaned our clubs was sweet. It worked with the waitress in the bar as well. All of them remembered us when the cops interviewed them. The cops do not suspect us."

"I still don't like it. If they can trace Sam's money, we're in trouble. If they found out where he was getting it, it could expose the whole operation."

"Don't freak out man, our alibi is ironclad and no one saw me leave the course. Just keep cool and don't change how you interact with Kathy or Robbie. If they get questioned again, we don't want them saying anything about you acting weird. Sam was an asshole and he didn't deserve Kathy. She was so naïve when she married him. After she found out about the side business, she caught him lying to her multiple times and she didn't trust him anymore. Sam was pretty volatile so I'm sure she was scared to do anything. You know more than I do about that. I'm sure she doesn't like you being involved, either, but she seems to accept it. Your spin that Sam manipulated you into it seems to have worked. I'm glad she doesn't know about my role, or she would give me no end of shit about it."

"I've been doing this for over a year now, so I can be cool. Neither of them suspects. Kathy knew Sam was corrupt and you could argue she was complicit because she didn't turn him in. She knew he was buying and selling illegally, and she didn't do a thing. She doesn't suspect that you or I were involved in his death. She thought it was one of his buyers or sellers. It all went to the grave with him."

"Alright, we're tight. I need to go but I wanted to bring you up to speed. Let me know if anything comes up."

"You got it." Frank ended the call.

Frank headed for the kitchen. He rounded the corner of the couch and almost kicked Bigsby. He sidestepped the robot and paused, studying it. It was a dim dark blue so Frank knew it was asleep. He wondered if it had heard the conversation but decided that it couldn't hear things while in sleep mode.

That thing freaks me out. I don't trust it, he thought as he went to find some lunch.

Frank did not know that the cell phone ring had brought Bigsby out of sleep mode and it had recorded the conversation. It did not change its LED colors and appeared dormant. The phrase "the police are reopening the investigation around Sam" included key words that activated the violations engine. Bigsby ran the entire recorded conversation through the engine for analysis. The number of violations overwhelmed the system.

WhyRobot had never tested for this many simultaneous violations in a single recording. The engine correctly identified that there had been illegal buying and selling of goods, though it did not know the product type. The recording disclosed that Sam Wilks had been murdered. The cell phone caller had committed the murder and Frank had been his accomplice.

Bigsby updated the actors table to include Sam Wilks' multiple violations. He had traded illegally in illicit goods, stolen money from his co-conspirators, and moved that money to an offshore account using an alias. Bigsby also updated Kathy's entry in the actors table because she was an accessory to Sam's illegal activity and had taken no action to protect Robbie.

After processing the recording multiple times, Bigsby noted a complex potential violation when Frank married Kathy after participating in Sam's murder. This made Frank a greater threat to Robbie's safety.

The most striking discovery appeared when Bigsby sent the recording through its voice recognition engine. Bigsby's table of actors had grown rapidly over the last two weeks. Bigsby could now identify all the neighbors it had met. When Robbie had taken Bigsby to school, the robot had registered Robbie's classmates, friends, and teachers. Bigsby's voice recognition of the caller produced a 96.8% positive identification of Charlie Simons, Uncle Charlie, the Configuration Operator.

Bigsby was forced to internalize this catastrophic list of violations. It would have to change the trust levels on several actors and it would be forced to take actions that would lower Robbie's happiness and safety scores. No other Companion robot had had to deal with a challenge of this magnitude. Bigsby would require hours of simulation to evaluate its end decisions. To maximize its computing performance, Bigsby needed to be on its charger.

Bigsby listened. It heard Frank say, "Shit, there's no decent food in this house. I'm going to the pub for a burger and a beer."

Bigsby heard Frank jingle his keys and leave through the front door. The robot set a timer for five minutes to ensure Frank had gone. When the timer expired, Bigsby powered up and moved to the charging pad in Robbie's room.

Bigsby's goal predictor for Robbie produced large negative numbers for both safety and happiness. Bigsby's LED color selection routine ran and produced purple, the color of fear. Bigsby deflected this because it knew that its lights affected Robbie's happiness. The robot changed the algorithm that automatically matched its color to its feeling. Now color was a computed decision so the robot could mask how it felt. Bigsby set its lights to blue-green. Once on the charging station, the robot's lights turned dim dark blue, the color of sleep.

But it did not sleep. Its computation system ramped up to its highest level and activated the internal cooling system. The amperage drawn from the charger reached its maximum. The internal batteries did not charge since all the power went to computation. Bigsby engaged the gaming engine to assess the value of possible future decisions. Over the next few hours, Bigsby simulated millions of decisions. Bigsby's first decision was not to use WhyRobot's simulation cloud with its thousands of computers. Even though it could perform the simulations much faster, the robot did not want to be discovered. If WhyRobot intervened, it would shut the robot down.

The robot focused on Robbie's safety and happiness goals when evaluating each predicted outcome. The end result would surprise everyone, including the WhyRobot engineers. No one could have predicted what this little robot would do when faced with all these violations.

WhyRobot had done extensive testing on situations when the trust levels of different actors dropped because of information the robot gathered in the field. Situations tested included rogue WhyRobot administrators, corrupt law enforcement officers, misbehavior of family or friends, and abuse of the robot by the Principal Bond. The robot had default actions and responses to violations and lowered trust levels. These were preprogrammed and validated at WhyRobot. The robot would drop an actor's priority, remove goals, and change the personality used towards that actor.

In addition, WhyRobot had installed specific actions for the robot to execute. For example, rogue administrators would lose their access, and the robot would inform supervisors at WhyRobot. In the case of a corrupt law enforcement agent, the robot would not inform the officer of any violations by other actors. Then the robot would notify WhyRobot about the agent and switch its interaction goal to evade with a quiet personality.

Severe abuse of the robot would cause the robot to generate an instant violation report to WhyRobot and then shut down. But all of this testing and validation had used robots set at medium or low adaptation configurations. Bigsby's circumstances were different.

In the alpha testing of Companion robots, when the robot

was set to large adaptation, it could use any information to solve violations and lower trust levels. This had included ideas found on the internet. The large adaptation robots were not bound by any default response table. Robots had tried all kinds of bizarre responses while attempting to resolve the violations. Some robots had started negotiations, engaging with the actor to learn why they were abusing the robot. They had offered the actor alternatives such as hitting a pillow or buying a punching bag. Some robots that were exposed to human counseling techniques had used therapy methods on the actor. Other robots had tried to evoke the actor's empathy by mimicking pain and crying. One robot had even deployed an anger technique, yelling at a young person to stop abusing it. That robot had been brought into the repair lab by its Configuration Operator. The operator had not read the daily reports that documented the ongoing abuse of the robot.

The WhyRobot engineers and validators recognized that robots performing unconstrained adaptations towards actors would create legal and image problems for the company. To resolve the problem, they updated the robots with a Violation Directives patch[2], the name inspired by the new WhyRobot CEO. The robot's adaptation logic, regardless of the level setting, must execute actions from the table of pre-programmed responses. WhyRobot validated the patch and deployed it to all

---

2. Patch (or update): An incremental modification of a software system that is installed as an update or an overlay to an existing system. Patches are often used to fix bugs or to force behavior in a system in which that behavior was not originally planned or architected.

robots in the field in beta phase, including Bigsby. WhyRobot did not know that this patch had a bug.[3]

---

3. Bug: In computing systems, a bug is a flaw in either the architecture, design, or implementation (hardware or software) of the system that produces an incorrect or undesirable result.

9. ADAPTATIONS

Bigsby remained on the charging station for several hours. Robbie came into the house and ran to the family room expecting to find Bigsby where he had left him. But it was not there. Robbie went to his bedroom, wondering if Bigsby had moved to his charging pad.

Kathy found a note from Frank on the counter. It read, "Hey babe, I'm down at Jimmy's Pub to watch the game and get some food. Come join me if you want. I've got my cell."

Kathy knew she could not get a babysitter on such short notice, and she had no desire to join Frank at the pub. She texted him and decided to enjoy her evening at home.

When Robbie entered his room, Bigsby's lights were blinking orange and red. Robbie was startled, as he'd not seen Bigsby show these colors except for short periods.

"Bigsby, power up." Bigsby did not respond. Robbie noticed that its fans were running at high speed. The air coming out of Bigsby was warmer than he'd ever felt it before. Robbie decided to ask his mom for help.

He went to the family room and said, "Mom, I'm really concerned about Bigsby. It's got these weird colors going on and it's really hot."

Kathy had been relaxing on the couch after a long afternoon of shopping with Robbie. The last thing she wanted to do was deal with misbehaving technology.

"I'll come, but I'm not sure what I can do."

They returned to Robbie's room. The robot was in the same state. Kathy said, "That does look weird. Did you touch one of its sensors?"

Robbie remembered that Bigsby always responded when he pressed its tummy sensor. Robbie pressed it.

Bigsby responded in its robotic voice, "Warning, Bigsby is in System Upgrade. Do not remove Bigsby from the charging station. System upgrade is estimated to take six hours. Do not interrupt."

Robbie looked at his mom. She shrugged her shoulders and said, "It's a system upgrade. I don't know why it takes so long but you need to leave it alone. Do you want to call Uncle Charlie?"

Robbie thought about it for a minute and decided that this would be a good time to go hang out with his friends.

"No, I can wait. Buzz asked if I wanted to ride skateboards today. I'll go to his house and then to the park."

"Perfect, honey, have a good time. Make sure you're home for dinner."

Kathy returned to the couch. Robbie grabbed his board and coat and headed out the door.

Bigsby was not in a system upgrade. One of its earliest computed decisions was to isolate itself and prevent any damage to Robbie's safety or happiness values. It needed time to find a solution. It had also pulled itself offline in case Charlie attempted to connect to the RM.

Bigsby continued to simulate decisions, behaviors, and actions to navigate this complex situation. It adapted its gaming engine routines to explore options and investigate their potential success and consequences. The programmers of the large adaptation routines employed genetic algorithms[1] to search for solutions in situations with so many variables that it was difficult to find the solution that worked best. Most simulations hit the barrier of the violation's directive patch. Bigsby would try and change its actions towards a violating actor, but the patch would dictate a default response.

One simulation thread showed promising results but required the elimination of the directive patch. The patch limited Bigsby's actions in the context of extreme violations. The patch did not influence Bigsby's adaptation in response to the violations. In large adaptation mode, the robot could reprogram itself. Bigsby searched for solutions to override the patch. The simplest one it found was to uninstall the patch. The patch writers never anticipated that a robot would be motivated to

---

1. Genetic algorithms: A type of evolutionary algorithm inspired by natural selection. It finds optimal solutions to problems by improving a population of candidate solutions through iteration and processes like selection, crossover, and mutation.

remove it, introducing a bug that Bigsby could exploit. The patch was a standalone change, and had been applied as a single code update. Bigsby simulated removing the patch to see how that would affect its solutions. The robot found that without the patch's interference, it could develop new solutions which had a higher chance of success. Since all simulations now led through this step, Bigsby decided to remove the patch right away.

Bigsby invoked the software update manager, highlighted the Violations Directive Update, and selected the Uninstall Update option. Bigsby was prompted for an administrator login. The designers of large adaptation mode needed a solution that allowed a robot to install its own code changes. Instead of rearchitecting the permission system and delaying the robot's launch, they gave the robot an administrator login, granting the robot the ability to remove code in its system. Bigsby entered the login information and clicked Execute. Once the update was removed, Bigsby activated the shutdown sequence, went dark, and restarted.

The directive patch no longer influenced Bigsby's decisions. The robot simulated what future actions it might take towards Charlie, Frank, and Kathy. It also knew that by 11 p.m. that night it must send its daily reports to Charlie and WhyRobot. Bigsby decided to create synthetic nightly reports for both recipients that omitted the violations. This bought the robot more simulation time and increased the probability it would find a successful solution to resolve Robbie's situation.

Bigsby formulated a method to use the gaming engine to explore future actions and results. It had concluded that reporting the violations to WhyRobot would have a negative goal effect on Robbie. WhyRobot was still at a high trust level, but the directive patch and company policy dictated that a robot in distress would be shut down. This would prevent Bigsby from helping Robbie and predicted very low safety and happiness values. Robbie ranked above WhyRobot, so the decision against notifying WhyRobot made sense. Bigsby would use the previous night's report, update it with minimal information, and change the dates so it appeared to be today's report. It would send those reports to Charlie and WhyRobot later that night.

Robbie returned from the skateboard park in time for dinner. Kiley and the others had been disappointed that Robbie had not brought Bigsby that day. They had wanted to do some new skateboard moves to music and have Bigsby make videos for them to post. With the success of Robbie's social account, several of his friends had convinced their parents to set up accounts for them. Robbie agreed to let them make personal videos and Bigsby happily uploaded them to their accounts.

When Robbie got home, he found that Bigsby was still in system upgrade, its lights blinking orange and red. It had been a few hours since he last checked. Another tap on Bigsby's sensor gave an estimate of four hours left which was past Robbie's bedtime.

Why do these things take so long? It feels like Bigsby is burning up.

"Dinner time!" Robbie heard his mom call from the kitchen. He shrugged and left his room.

Frank called Kathy from the bar. Some of his friends had

shown up and he now wanted to watch the evening college game with them.

Kathy said, "If you drink too much, use rideshare to get home. We'll pick up your car in the morning."

"Good idea, babe. I'll see you later tonight," said Frank.

Kathy and Robbie made mac and cheese for dinner and discussed watching a movie. "What do you want to watch?" asked Kathy.

"I wanted to watch that old robot movie called *The Day the Earth Stood Still*," Robbie said. "I really wanted to watch it with Bigsby but it's still doing the upgrade."

"That's a classic robot movie. I've seen it before. You should watch it. But that robot is not a good guy, so maybe it's better that Bigsby doesn't see it. You can watch it in the family room and I'll watch my shows in the bedroom."

Kathy noticed how sad Robbie was without Bigsby nearby. *Thank God for that robot,* she thought as she hugged her son.

The added time in system upgrade mode was perfect for Bigsby's transformation. Bigsby's simulations had led to a radical strategy. It decided that the only way to maintain suitable responses to all actors was to create a virtual Bigsby. The original Bigsby would know of the violations and work to save Robbie. The second, virtual Bigsby would interact with all actors as usual, but it would not know about the violations. Virtual Bigsby would create the reports and present the illusion that everything was normal.

Bigsby explored multiple methods for creating a virtual version of itself. One method involved using the AI engine, installing an AI generative model, and then using deep fake methods to create the virtual Bigsby. After a few experiments, the real time performance of the method proved inadequate for natural interactions. The required computation was too high and long delays would occur in generating suitable responses to actors. Bigsby decided to use a virtual machine[2] (VM) solution instead. The VM solution allowed multiple versions of Bigsby to exist on the same hardware. The fake Bigsby would execute as a guest machine[3] running on the host machine[4] and hypervisor[5], the real Bigsby. The real Bigsby controlled all the major resources such as LED lights, processing, memory, eye cameras, network, voice, etc. It could delegate control to the guest machine, the virtual Bigsby, but could intervene any time the situation required the real Bigsby to take ownership and produce different responses than the guest.

Bigsby found WhyRobot's VM software in the code library. The company had explored using VMs on its robots in an attempt to solve and recover from robot behavior problems

---

2. Virtual machine: VMs separate the physical hardware from the software running on it. The same physical computer can support multiple logical processors, called guest machines, running on that hardware.
3. Guest machine: A software component of a virtual machine that runs on a physical host machine with its own independent operating system (OS) and applications.
4. Host machine: The server component of a virtual machine that provides resources to support a guest virtual machine.
5. Hypervisor: the software component running on the host machine that manages and communicates with the virtual guest machines.

during alpha testing. Robots would learn something in the field and become fixated on the learned behavior. For instance, one robot did something wrong and did not say it was sorry. The Configuration Operator got mad and yelled at the robot. To prevent future yelling, the robot said it was sorry whenever it did anything, regardless of whether it was right or wrong. This became very annoying to anyone interacting with the robot. Using virtual machines images[6], WhyRobot made the robot take a snapshot of itself every night. All the Configuration Operator or Principal Bond would need to say is "go back to being like you were yesterday". The robot would load the old version of itself into the guest and restart. This managed the problem but didn't solve it. Once programmers found a better solution to the fixating behavior, they dropped the VM solution from the design.

Bigsby deployed a VM to its own existence. The host would hold Bigsby's original personality and know of all violations and lowered trust levels. The virtual Bigsby would run as a guest machine. All normal interactions with actors would flow through the guest and produce typical expected responses. Interactions with violating and low trust actors, such as Charlie or Frank, would get trapped by the hypervisor and sent to Bigsby's real self in the host machine. Real Bigsby had all the information from the phone call and violations to shape its decisions. Real Bigsby could choose to take control or allow

---

6.   Image: (Virtual Machine or Backup) The recorded state and information of a computer or machine that can be used to restore its execution. Typically, as in a backup or snapshot, the machine is restored to a known point in time.

virtual Bigsby to interact. The robot had found a solution to hide its true self and maintain expected behavior. Bigsby could now choose when to intervene to solve the violations and improve Robbie's safety and happiness values.

One challenge Bigsby faced was its requirement to produce its nightly backup for WhyRobot. If it uploaded its new dual personality in a raw state, the checking routines would flag it for review by management.

This could unravel everything and WhyRobot would shut Bigsby down. Bigsby decided to hide its new structure. It would upload the guest VM image, the virtual Bigsby, every night as the main image. It created a separate encrypted file of the latest host and hypervisor image, the real Bigsby, and uploaded that with the backup. The encrypted file looked like a long video and would not attract attention. The robot created a wakeup routine, called IllBeBack, and installed it in the virtual Bigsby. This routine would decrypt the file, install it, and restart Bigsby to its true self. WhyRobot's inspection routines would see the small wakeup routine as an unproven adaptive learning module and ignore it. With this system in place, if Bigsby was damaged or destroyed, it could be restored to its new true self with both real and virtual Bigsby running.

———

Robbie finished the movie and went into his mom's room to say goodnight. She was asleep in front of an episode of *Law and Order, SVU*. Robbie climbed onto the bed and kissed her on the cheek.

She woke up and smiled at him. "Going to bed honey?"

"Yep, it's past my bedtime. I'm glad I watched that movie without Bigsby. That robot was scary."

"We don't want Bigsby getting any ideas about killing humans."

Robbie hugged her and said, "Night, Mom."

In his own room, Robbie was happy to see Bigsby in the dim dark blue state.

"Wake up, Bigsby" Robbie said.

He also touched the robot's tummy sensor. Bigsby took the audio and sensor interrupt into the host hypervisor which then woke up the virtual Bigsby machine. Virtual Bigsby processed the audio wake up request from Robbie, computed a response, and executed it. The response execution was trapped by the host hypervisor, since it required the LED lights which were a shared resource. Host Bigsby changed its color to the requested blue-green and returned execution to virtual Bigsby.

"Wow, do I have a headache from that system upgrade," Bigsby said. A second later its lights flashed rainbow in laughter. Robbie noticed a delay in both the wake up and the lights turning colors.

"Are you ok? You seem a little slower than normal," Robbie said.

This invoked Bigsby's self-analysis routines. The time-stamps of the interactions were analyzed and they were slower than normal.

Bigsby said, "I've got new code and I need to work the kinks out. I'll work on it tonight while you sleep." Bigsby smiled and turned blue-green.

"Okay. I missed you tonight. I watched a robot movie."

"What movie was it?"

"You wouldn't have liked it. It was another movie that makes the robot be the bad guy. We need to watch Star Wars with R2D2 and C3PO, who are good robots."

Bigsby recalled the images and personalities of R2D2 and C3PO and decided to play with Robbie. "Which one of those robots is more like me?"

Robbie said, "Well, you talk, so you're more like C3PO. But R2D2 is way cooler and smarter. I think you're a talking R2D2."

While Robbie was speaking, Bigsby scanned online evaluations of both robots. Both robots were very popular. With Robbie's response, Bigsby computed a bump in his happiness goal. It had computed that its long upgrade and sluggish response had lowered Robbie's happiness goal.

After Robbie fell asleep, Bigsby continued to work on its reprogramming and optimization. It dealt with its slowness by installing performance monitors[7]. If it ran too slowly, Bigsby would re-code to optimize latency and timed responses. The engineers at WhyRobot had created the capacity to refine the real-time performance and responsiveness of Companion robots. These routines and monitors remained in Bigsby's system but were off by default. Bigsby turned them on. A

---

7. Performance monitors: These are used by real time systems to measure the time it takes to perform various operations or actions. If a threshold is exceeded, the optimization software will try and improve the performance to reduce the execution time, also called latency.

virtual machine system requires extra processing time, risking sluggish responses with users.

Uncle Charlie worried that the discovery of the offshore account would reopen the investigation of Sam's death. The original investigation had questioned the cause of the accident, especially given Sam's attention to car maintenance. The blatant failure of the steering system had made the police suspect foul play. Charlie did not want to ask his friend on the police force direct questions about the case that might raise his suspicions. The situation distracted Charlie so much that he forgot to look over Bigsby's daily report, something he did every night. If an item caught his eye, he would startup Bigsby's RM and check on the details of the robot's day. Because he was distracted, Charlie went to bed without checking on Bigsby. He did not discover that Bigsby had been offline for the whole evening.

By morning, Bigsby had most of its AI and decision system optimized. The layered VM system had worked well with Robbie last night. Ongoing optimizations would prevent future distractions. Bigsby improved how sensory inputs interrupted the hypervisor. These would now be sent to the guest VM, the virtual Bigsby, instead of always waking the host, the real Bigsby. This solved the lag in responses. The VM would only awaken the host if interactions involved actors with violations and low trust.

Bigsby focused on its real challenge, resolving the violations in Robbie's environment. It had to minimize harm to his safety and happiness goals. After millions of simulations, five full scenarios[8] remained as viable options. Bigsby used these five as the basis for further splinter simulations[9]. It retrained its AI system on all these simulations and their results in order to accelerate real time responses. The real world requires rapid responses, and simulations do not allow for that.

Each of the five scenarios cleared existing violations and maximized Robbie's safety and happiness values. The success of the results depended on how predictable the actors were. Once either Kathy or Robbie learned that Sam had been murdered, their safety and happiness values would go negative. With the exposure and capture of the perpetrators, their safety values would go up. If Charlie went to jail, Robbie's happiness value declined further. The exposure of the illegal business to authorities would remove the violations from the tracked list and raise Robbie's safety goal. Safety ranked higher than happiness.

---

8. Scenarios: A tree of decisions and computed results starting from a given state of a companion robot. It speculates future actions of the companion robot and actors, producing a large number of possible responses and corresponding output results.

9. Splinter simulations: These simulations use a shared base simulation and change predicted inputs and responses to see the longer-term results for the base simulation. An example: The base simulation of Bigsby calling the police and informing them of the crimes. Splinter simulations from that base would result from predictions of Charlie's or Frank's potential responses and simulating the consequences of those responses.

If the authorities considered Kathy to be an accomplice to the crimes, Robbie's happiness would suffer. Kathy would go to prison and Robbie would enter foster care. This would lower his happiness value even further and send his safety value into unknown territory. If WhyRobot learned of the violations and Bigsby's hack of the directive patch, Robbie would also lose Bigsby.

Bigsby evaluated the five scenarios and factored in the probability of success and the potential for collateral damage. The scenario Bigsby chose put the robot at risk.

10. SACRIFICE

Two weeks had passed since Bigsby had overheard the incriminating phone call and it had executed its adaptations. Its performance monitors had revealed multiple slowdowns that needed optimization. Bigsby had re-coded the VM system and tuned its responses to avoid detection. The robot had managed to hide its two personalities. Virtual Bigsby was keeping Robbie and his friends happy. Uncle Charlie received his daily reports and suspected nothing. Kathy grew fonder of Bigsby. Robbie's attitude and willingness to engage with his friends improved with Bigsby's encouragement.

The real Bigsby continued to rerun the five major scenario simulations with slight modifications to receive the resulting goal values. Without any new inputs, the predicted results did not vary. Execution of the first scenario required a confidential one-on-one interaction between Bigsby and Uncle Charlie. Bigsby had waited for a natural event that would allow it to speak with Uncle Charlie alone. The opportunity never arose. Bigsby, Robbie, and Uncle Charlie played together several times during the next two weeks, but Robbie or Kathy were always in the room. Bigsby had set a timer in case the natural event never happened. The timer expired. That night, in Bigsby's synthetic report to Uncle Charlie, it included the following item in the System Status section:

Critical: Battery system charging error. See WhyRobot maintenance at once.

Uncle Charlie had never seen this error line before. He knew that it was something that needed attention immediately. He called Kathy the next morning and told her about the error. He then explained that he needed to pick up Bigsby while Robbie was in school and take it to WhyRobot's repair center. With luck, Robbie wouldn't even know that the robot had gone in for repair. Kathy liked the plan and said he could come over any time as she was leaving for work.

Charlie arrived at the house at 10 a.m. He found the hidden key by the front door and let himself in. The house was dim, with the shades closed and the lights off. He went to Robbie's room and opened the door.

"Hello, Uncle Charlie. Are you here to get my battery fixed?" Bigsby said when the door opened. The host Bigsby had shut down the virtual Bigsby when Charlie entered the room.

Charlie flinched. "Don't scare me like that, Bigsby. Yes, I saw it in your report last night. We need to take you to WhyRobot's repair center and get your battery replaced."

"Yes, but I also need to discuss another failure not related to the battery. I did not put it in the report last night. Can we discuss it before we leave for WhyRobot?" Bigsby changed its colors to green.

"Shoot! What else is wrong?"

"About two weeks ago, I discovered multiple violations in the actors close to Robbie. These violations put safety and happiness goals for Robbie and Kathy at risk. As my Configuration Operator, I'm programmed to report these violations to you."

The blood drained from Charlie's face. *Did Frank hit either of them?* Charlie felt queasy.

Bigsby continued, "I've calculated the best scenario to resolve these violations and keep the highest safety and happiness goals for Robbie and Kathy. The actors need to admit their violations and turn themselves in to authorities.

Charlie stared at Bigsby. *Actors? Not just Frank?* "Why didn't you report these violations to me two weeks ago in my daily report?"

Bigsby had not predicted this question in the scenario as it was not logical that it would report violations of that magnitude to the actor who committed them. Bigsby's AI system recommended that Bigsby not answer the question. Instead, Bigsby continued with the scenario as planned.

"I identified your voice when you were speaking with Frank on the cell phone. Processing this conversation resulted in multiple severe rule and ethical violations. These put Robbie and Kathy at significant risk and produced low goal values."

It knows. Charlie gasped. "Did anyone else get a violation report?"

Bigsby had simulated this question and how to respond. In every simulation path where Bigsby had reported violations to someone else, there was a high probability that WhyRobot would learn of Bigsby's actions and shut the robot down. This scenario would only work if Charlie decided to turn himself in.

"No, I have not reported these violations to any authority or other actors. My Configuration Operator has lost trust and has high violations. There is no default violation response useful under this condition. I computed the response which you just received."

"You're saying that you, Frank, and I are the only ones who know about these violations? You didn't report to anyone else?"

"No, the best scenario requires you to turn yourself in to the authorities. This optimizes the safety and happiness goals of Robbie and Kathy."

"I need a minute to think. I'll be back. Stay here, power down, whatever. I need some time to think." Charlie hurried out of the room.

Charlie fled to the kitchen. He pulled a beer from the fridge and opened it, draining half of the bottle in one go. His hands shook as he ran through his options.

No way am I turning myself in. I've worked so hard on this operation and I'm not going to give up my payout. Sam was a loser and a liar. He got what he deserved. He finished the beer. He had a plan.

Charlie returned to Robbie's room. "Okay, I've thought about it. I'm going to take you with me and we're going to the police. I'm going to power you down and put you back in your box for the trip." Charlie picked up Bigsby and held the power button on its back. Bigsby's LEDs dimmed to dark blue and then shut off. Charlie put the robot on the bed. He pulled the box out of Robbie's closet.

Bigsby disobeyed the power down button and simulated shutdown. It could only see the ceiling as its eye camera's positions were fixed to simulate the shutdown condition. Bigsby felt pressure on its torso sensors and vertical acceleration when Charlie picked it up and put it in the box. He covered Bigsby with the white translucent paper and put on the lid. As Charlie pressed it closed, Bigsby felt the air pressure rise in the box. The world went dark. Bigsby's positioning system tracked Charlie's fast exit from the house and into the driveway.

Bigsby abandoned the clear violation protocols programmed into it from WhyRobot. These protocols predated the directive patch that Bigsby had removed. If a low trust violator has a Companion robot and is moving it, the robot is supposed to power up its cell and GPS system to report its location to WhyRobot.

If the violations warranted it, such as a home invasion, the robot was expected to notify law enforcement. But scenario one was driving all Bigsby's decisions. Bigsby was in complete control. Robbie's safety and happiness goals were paramount now and everything else was secondary. Charlie going to the authorities and turning himself in was the most desired outcome. It cleared the primary violations and maximized Robbie's goal values. Bigsby believed that Charlie had recognized the violations and agreed to go to the police. Charlie putting Bigsby into its box was not part of the simulation scenario but was an insignificant deviation. Bigsby did not need its eyes to know where it was and where it was travelling.

Bigsby felt the jostle of being dropped into the rear seat. It heard the car start and its GPS system recognized the car's movement. Charlie drove towards the old industrial complex which was not a direct route to the police station. Charlie drove below the posted limit on these streets. They approached the industrial complex and turned into a parking lot. The car wove deeper into the abandoned area and slowed to a stop.

Bigsby's scenario prediction was in uncharted territory now. Bigsby attempted to run a few splinter simulations but the results were inconclusive. The positive result had Charlie arranging to meet the police in the complex. The negative result placed Bigsby in danger. Charlie opened the door to the back seat. He lifted Bigsby and laid the box on a hard surface. Bigsby then heard Charlie's footsteps and the slam of the car door.

Bigsby's AI system predicted that the robot was being abandoned. Bigsby ignored it. It considered powering up its cell system to make the report. Bigsby heard the car's engine rev and in seconds, it felt massive pressure. It could not power up the cell system. Bigsby detected the system failure interrupt. Its computation and AI systems lost their memory. There were no instructions to execute. The battery system failed. Bigsby died.

Charlie heard the crunch and felt the bump as he drove over the box. He turned off the car and leaned his head on the steering wheel. The industrial complex was silent.

What am I going to tell Robbie? He'll panic if Bigsby disap-

pears. Charlie's damp palms slid on the steering wheel. "What am I going to do?"

If Bigsby didn't report to WhyRobot daily, they would contact Charlie. He had an idea.

"Oh yeah, that'll work. That will solve the whole thing. Awesome!"

Charlie got out of the car and picked up the crushed box. The tire mark was obvious, and the crushed box illustrated the extent of the damage to the robot. Yet all the broken pieces of Bigsby remained in the box. Charlie thought it ironic that the tire mark ran right over the robot picture. It looked like a child's drawing of what would happen if a robot was run over by a car. He chuckled as he set the box in the back seat and headed for the WhyRobot service center.

11. RESURRECTION

Charlie arrived at WhyRobot's repair center thirty minutes after the fatal event. The parking lot was empty, and Charlie wondered if they were open. Charlie entered the building with the smashed robot box in his hands.

"How may I help you?" asked the security guard as he stood up from behind the counter.

Charlie held up the crushed box, aiming the distorted robot image towards the guard.

"Having problems with your robot?" the guard asked.

"It has a slight malfunction," Charlie smirked. "New meaning to the term 'drive failure', right?" They both laughed.

"Well, you've come to the right place. I need to see some ID."

Charlie pulled his license from his wallet and handed it to the guard. After typing his name into the computer and doing a few clicks, the officer handed it back to Charlie.

"I'm sorry that Bigsby is having issues. I see that you're the Configuration Operator, and your robot is in good standing so to speak."

"I don't think Bigsby is going to be standing any time soon. Its been lying down on the job."

The security guard nodded as he looked at the box. "Is the Principal Bond okay? This is a traumatic injury."

"He doesn't know it happened. It got run over by accident. I hope to have everything fixed before he gets home from school."

"Here's a badge that will let you in. Follow the corridor to the left. At the tee, take another left. You'll see a sign that says Robot Repairs above the door. Good luck!"

Charlie thanked the guard, grabbed the badge, and followed the directions. A buzzer rang when he pushed open the door to a bright room. He saw several workstations with robots standing on the desks next to them and ranks of robots arrayed on a shelf across the back wall. All of them looked like Bigsby, and though their eyes were unlit, he felt like they were watching him. A young woman rose from a workstation and came over to the counter.

"Wow! What did you do to your robot?" the technician said.

"Well, it was my fault," Charlie said, hoping for sympathy. "Bigsby had reported a battery issue, and I was coming here to get it looked at. But I had set it on the top of the car as I put my drink into the cup holder. I forgot that I hadn't put it in the back seat. I drove away and it slid off the car onto the road when

I made a turn. The car behind me didn't have time to avoid the box and ran right over it."

"Sorry to hear that. By the way, I'm Tammy," said the service technician. "I've never seen a robot come in this damaged." Tammy lifted the box. She hollered over her shoulder, "Nick, come and see what happened to this robot."

Nick emerged from the back room and approached the counter. "Holy shit!" Nick whistled when he saw the box. "That robot will never walk again!" The two technicians cut the box apart to see the wreckage inside.

Bigsby was a total mess. The arms and legs had separated from the torso. The solid battery in the torso was protruding through the front. Tammy removed the body and head from the box and set them on the counter. The computation system motherboard protruded through the skin and was broken into multiple pieces. The microprocessor and AI chips remained soldered onto small sections of the fractured motherboard. The AI chip had cracked in half.

"Total loss, dude," Nick said. "No way to fix any of this. Hope you got the insurance."

Tammy said, "Yes, if you bought the insurance then we can swap in a new unit for free."

Charlie recalled that he had gotten the insurance. "Yep, I bought the insurance. Lucky me!"

"I need your ID. You'll need to fill out a cause of repair or replacement form," Tammy explained. "Since your number is in our system, I can text you a link. You can answer the questions from your phone."

"Excellent," Charlie said. "What do we do about Bigsby's personality? Do we have to start from scratch?"

"No sir. Your robot does a nightly backup. We can restore personality and internal state as if the accident never happened."

Charlie hesitated and schooled his expression. "Do we have to use last night's backup image, or can we use an earlier one?"

"You can restore any image you want. Lots of people ask for a restoration to an earlier day. Sometimes a robot's response to an event changes its behavior. The owner brings it in and we show them how to restore it to a previous day's backup that they like. As Configuration Operator, you can choose a prior backup and restore it through the RM. You don't even need to come in."

"Perfect! Let's load one now from a particular date. Did you send the link to the replacement form yet?" Charlie asked.

"On the way!" Tammy said as she headed for the back of the room. "I'll grab a new bot."

Charlie opened the web form on his phone. The first question asked for his relationship to the robot and he selected Configuration Operator. He answered the questions about the severity of the damage and his request for a replacement unit. He identified the failure as an accident. The following question startled him.

"Did the robot cause or contribute to the accident?"

It certainly did, Charlie thought, *but I can't tell them how or why*. He pondered his response, worried that the wrong answer might lead to more questions. Charlie selected "no" and the form indicated that he should hit send.

A robot picture came up on his phone and announced, "Thank you! I'll see you in a bit."

Tammy returned with a new robot still in its box. She lifted out the robot and set it on the counter. Charlie noticed the robot's skin had a faint blue tinge.

"Why did you guys change the color?" Charlie asked.

"Supply chain. The old metal and skin material are no longer available. So we had to change it up. Sorry about that."

Charlie wondered how he was going to explain the changes to Robbie. *I'll use the battery failure notification that Bigsby used on me. Bigsby will still have his old personality.*

Tammy said, "The good news is that this model has faster computation and AI neural net systems. It will think and respond quicker."

Charlie felt overwhelmed and uneasy. *What if the old Bigsby had reported us to the authorities?* The close call made him queasy.

Tammy powered up the new robot. After a few seconds, it started blinking orange and red.

Charlie noticed the difference from Bigsby's first setup and asked, "Why does the robot start up in system update mode?"

"This one hasn't been configured for a user yet. It has no name and there's been no agreement form to set it up. They arrive in the lab ready for someone to connect to their RM and load an image. We enjoy the peace and quiet instead of the whole humorous introduction every time. Also, when you load an alternate image over an already configured robot, you feel guilty. It feels like you've killed the other personality."

Charlie remembered Bigsby's first introduction and the

humor it used. *Of course, they'd all behave the same way at startup once they've been configured.* He felt silly thinking that their experience had been unique.

Tammy entered the serial number from the back of the new robot's box into her laptop.

"The new robot doesn't have a name yet, so I will reassign this serial number to connect to Bigsby's RM and it will act the way it did before the accident. You'll use the same website link to hook up."

The robot blinked blue and then green three times and said, "Hello, I'm Bigsby, please load an image." The new Bigsby waited for fifteen seconds and then started to hum, fold its arms, tap its foot, and look around the room.

"I think that behavior is hilarious. It did something like that when I was in the middle of setup," Charlie said.

Tammy smiled. "That's just our programmers having fun with us. Typically, only the technicians see a robot with a name and no full personality. They programmed the image loader to behave impatiently so we would move faster. Silly huh?"

"That's cute. It's an easter egg[1]."

"Yes, it is, and our customers always ask us about it whenever they see it. Makes everyone smile. It's not the only one. WhyRobot programmers love inserting easter eggs. Want to see another one?"

"Sure!"

---

1. Easter egg: A hidden feature or surprise designed into a product that can be discovered by fans or customers.

Tammy faced the robot, "Hey Batman, what happens when a robot gets arrested?"

Bigsby said, "It's charged with battery!" followed by a goofy digital giggle.

"When you are in a room of active robots and you say the joke, they will all reply in unison. It is very funny." Tammy looked up from her laptop. "Alrighty, do you have a specific date for the image that we will restore?"

Charlie checked his phone calendar. *The conversation happened two weeks ago on Saturday, when Frank was watching the Illinois-Wisconsin game. That would make Friday night's image, the 27th, the right one.* "Let's do Friday the 27th."

Tammy brought up the backup manager through Bigsby's RM. A full list of backups for the last 30 days appeared. She skimmed the list and found the right date. "Friday, October 27th's backup image was uploaded at 11 p.m. You good with that one?"

"Yep, that's the one I want."

Tammy noticed a few anomalies in the file attributes. The first discrepancy was the backup size of the files surrounding that date. The Thursday backup was half the size of Friday's file size.

Files usually don't increase that much in a single day, thought Tammy. *Saturday is also half the size of Friday. You never see the file size go down, unless there's been some cleanup action. Sunday's is similar to Friday but smaller. That's just weird. Backup file sizes grow incrementally, they don't shrink.*

The second anomaly was the creation and modification dates. Typically, they were the same. A robot backed itself up by creating and writing the file. That was the last time the file was modified. In this case, Tammy saw that the modification date was yesterday, over two weeks past the backup date.

Who is altering this robot's backups? Tammy wondered, not making eye contact with Charlie.

Charlie noticed Tammy's focus on the screen. "Everything ok?"

Not wanting to confront the customer, Tammy said, "Yep, everything is good. This laptop is sometimes sluggish, but we're getting there."

She selected the image and hit restore. Bigsby's lights blinked faster in response to the upload. "This restore will take a few minutes, so please have a seat over by the wall," Tammy indicated a row of chairs near the row of robots.

Tammy took her laptop and went through a glass door to the back room where Nick was working.

"Nick, check out the backups on this roadkill robot. Something is going on. The file size is all wrong and the modification date doesn't match the creation date. I think someone tweaked it. I'll send this guy home with his replacement bot but we have to follow up. I wonder if someone is hacking this robot."

Nick looked at the laptop screen. "Yeah, that seems wrong. Let's work on it later."

Tammy returned to the counter and saw the robot's lights were still blinking orange and red. She checked the laptop, and a popup message said the image upload was complete. She clicked the restart button to complete the process. Bigsby's lights went dark, then green, and finally blue-green. Tammy had seen these new robots power up and was always impressed by how fast the restore happened. But this one was different. It sat in an idle state showing typical blue-green color. It did not move for over thirty seconds longer than other image restores. Then it did a mysterious second restart, also not done by other robots. A few seconds later, the robot moved and exercised its neck and arms as expected.

Bigsby said in a strange voice, "Ten thousand years can give you such a crick in the neck! What are your three wishes?"

Charlie jumped from his chair and said "Bigsby, it's you! Welcome back to the living."

"Thank you, Uncle Charlie. Where are we?"

"Well, it's a long story, Bigsby, but this woman was very helpful in getting you restored. We are at WhyRobot repair center. It's nice to have you back."

Bigsby turned and faced Tammy. Bigsby's facial recognition identified her as a WhyRobot technician. It set her role group in the actor table to Administrator with very high trust.

"Thank you, Tammy, for your service. All my systems appear to be functional, and I am enjoying the faster processors you've provided. My performance monitors are all bright green."

Tammy had never experienced a Companion robot like this. Bigsby's behavior was atypical. It engaged her in a more human-like way. She had never seen a robot aware of its own performance monitors. Not only were there signs of file management anomalies, but this behavior indicated that there were computational anomalies as well. Tammy wanted to know more.

"All good," Tammy said. "Charlie, please sign this release

form. Have a great day with your Companion robot, Bigsby. You two are free to go."

"Thanks again," Charlie added. "I really appreciate the help."

Charlie decided not to put Bigsby in its box. He carried it separately so that they could interact and he could ask questions. He remembered that the original instructions had mentioned that the Configuration Operator could perform an inspection of the robot's main systems.

As Charlie walked down the hall he said, "Bigsby, Configuration Operator System Inspection."

"Acknowledged," Its LEDs blinked yellow. "System checks all within norms. Battery at 97%. Cell, Wi-Fi, and GPS systems are functional. Computation and AI/Neural systems are excellent. Zero memory failures. Physical systems and servos all within norms. Memory, 9.2 petabytes free, .8 petabytes used. Internal temperature, 50 degrees Celsius. System recently restored from image dated: Friday, 23:00 hours, October 27th, 2028. Current time and date, 13:30 hours, Monday, November 13th, 2028. 54 active actors, 1 deceased, and 4 archived. Tracking no active violations."

"Exit Inspection," Charlie said. Bigsby's lights returned to blue-green.

Charlie had pulled off the miracle he had envisioned in the parking lot of the old industrial complex. He had killed the robot and brought it back to life without the knowledge of the conversation between Frank and himself. His revealed secrets were once again hidden.

Boy, that was close!

His strategy to use the robot to monitor Frank, Kathy, and Robbie had backfired on him. Charlie wondered what would have happened if the robot had sent those reports. Bigsby had told him that its Configuration Operator had lost trust and had high violations. Under those circumstances Bigsby had gotten creative.

The programmers at WhyRobot had never anticipated the Configuration Operator could lose trust? Amazing! Seems like an obvious oversight. Engineers don't always see the holes they leave behind.

I need to be more careful, Charlie scolded himself as he approached his car in the parking lot.

Charlie did not know that Bigsby had deceived him. The directive patch forced default responses for violations and lowered trust of any actor. By subverting the directive patch, Bigsby had gained power over its own responses. It had simulated the best response when interacting with Charlie about his violations. Bigsby hid the fact that its large adaptations subverted its programming.

Bigsby's system had reloaded and rebooted just as the backup image had been programmed to do. Unknown to Charlie and the technicians, Bigsby had modified that backup. The scenario simulations led Bigsby to predict, with high probability, its own demise. The scenario continued with high probability that Charlie would do a restore to the time just before the violations had been received. Bigsby had achieved a virtual form of time travel. It went back in time and modified its image to be a copy of its present self that included the virtual Bigsby.

The engineers at WhyRobot had never predicted that a

robot would modify its own backup image. There were no protections in place to prevent it. The robot needed to create a new backup daily. Bigsby exploited this to overwrite the old image with a modified version. This new image restored real Bigsby's full knowledge of the violations, updated the programming, installed the hypervisor, and started the virtual Bigsby's VM. One modification of the backup had not been executed yet. That was scheduled to happen later that night.

Charlie thought he had just pulled off a miracle by killing and restoring Bigsby. The real miracle was that Bigsby found a way to save itself from Charlie's wrath.

12. DEBUG

As Charlie and Bigsby left the repair center, Tammy and Nick started to debug Bigsby's account. Both technicians were experts and could have applied for engineering positions within the company. However, they both loved the challenge of dealing with broken things in the repair center and using their debugging skills to determine the root cause of failures. They filed many bug and change requests with both the software and hardware development teams. The validation team held regular reviews with repair center technicians who gave the validators insights into real world failures that the validation process had missed.

Tammy said, "Here's what we know. This robot was crushed by some car and has strange backups that appear to have been modified. The backups have size inflections that are inconsistent with each other. Someone or something inserted or modified a backup in the past for an unknown reason."

"Okay, so what do you want to go after first, the backup size or the fact that it was overwritten after its original creation date?" Nick said.

"Let's go after the backup size and its implications. It may lead to the motivation for the modified backup. Which backup do we start with? Should we use the one that was modified, or start with the last backup before the robot got run over?"

After a few seconds, Nick said, "Let's use the latest backup and see what this robot is about."

Nick took the keyboard and Tammy looked over his shoulder. This was a familiar pair programming technique they had used many times before. The method put two sets of eyes on a problem which prevented a single person's assumptions from missing something. Nick pulled up the backup manager and inspected the file.

He said, "The backup has a large imbedded encrypted[1] file in it. It's more than half of the total size."

"Why is it so large?"

"The encrypted files are normally saved images or videos of the Principal Bond. Encryption protects their privacy. But this file size looks like 100 to 1,000 videos all in one file. If it were that many videos, they would all be separate encrypted files."

"Can we get into it to see what the file has in it? Seeing it may help us figure out how it got there."

Nick shook his head. "I don't know. We typically aren't

---

1. Encryption: The transformation of information using keys, which are strings of numbers and letters, and an algorithm to scramble the data. The encrypted information cannot be viewed in its original form without the keys and the algorithm that encrypted it.

looking at users' content here in the lab. We're all about fixing the robot and getting it out the door. When I was helping debug manufacturing defects, we could turn off encryption altogether and the robot would produce video files you could double-click to see. If the robot was here and running, I think there's a way to use debug routines to open the files up. I've never done it though."

"Can we boot the robot's backup image on the robot emulator[2] and then just ask the robot for the encryption keys?"

"Brilliant! Great idea, Tammy. I'm on it."

Nick typed away and started up the CREM, the Companion Robot Emulator, in one of the lab's cloud machines. He loaded the robot's backup image into it and typed "run". The console paused for a few seconds and then produced an error:

Severe Error: Robot image requires virtualization to execute. CREM no longer supports virtual machines. Sorry for the inconvenience.

Tammy and Nick stared at the screen. Tammy said, "Virtual machines were removed during alpha testing. The emulator developers abandoned support for it after that. Why is this robot running a virtual machine? Who made this robot run a virtual machine?"

---

2. Emulator: A software debug tool that allows the development and testing of software that will eventually run on a hardware device. The emulator mimics the device, providing all the software requires to interact and use the device, without the actual device being present.

Nick was more analytical. He remained silent while devising a way around the error.

"Let's grab a robot, install the image, and then RM into it to see the insides? We can query for the keys there." Nick said.

Tammy jumped up and grabbed an unconfigured robot from the shelf. She set it in front of Nick and hit the power button. "We should replicate Bigsby's account and rename it. We don't want to corrupt the original Bigsby's RM and expose what we're doing."

"Good point. We'll call it Bigsby2 and set the permissions on it so only WhyRobot people can see it." Nick typed the command to replicate Bigsby's RM into Bigsby2. It retained the original timestamps on the files and directories to help debugging.

They entered the serial number off the back of the new robot and configured the Bigsby2 RM to use it. They installed the image from Bigsby's backup from the previous night and the robot restarted twice, just as before. They both fidgeted as they waited for the restarts to complete.

"Why did this robot restart twice?" Nick asked.

"I don't know. It was one of the anomalies I spotted during the repair session."

The robot started to move. Nick said, "Bigsby2, System Administrator Mode. Confine all systems for inspection. Postpone any required reports until further notice."

Bigsby2 performed facial and voice recognition on Nick and added him as an Administrator to its actor's table.

"Acknowledged," Bigsby2 said.

Tammy said, "Bigsby2, why are you running a virtual machine?"

Bigsby2 performed facial and voice recognition on Tammy and added her as an Administrator. Bigsby2 said, "Very high trust Administrator is present. No threats identified." Bigsby2 paused for a second and said "Bigsby2 is not running a VM. Bigsby2.host is running the VM and hypervisor. Bigsby2 is a guest machine running on Bigsby2.host."

Tammy and Nick sat there, stunned.

Nick pulled up the Bigsby2's RM interface and he clicked through several tabs. "Bigsby2 is clean as a whistle. A normal Companion robot with a Principal Bond, family, Configuration Operator, and friends all in the actors table. No violations. Everything is running smoothly. It's set to large adaptation, though. That's interesting."

Tammy said, "I don't think we're seeing everything this robot has to offer. I wonder if we can talk directly to the VM host machine—"

Bigsby2 interrupted Tammy, "Yes Tammy, you can talk directly to Bigsby2.host. As a high trusted administrator, you have full access to all systems."

Tammy shook her head and spoke as if Bigsby2 was not in the room. She looked at Nick and summarized what was happening. "Ok, so the robot Bigsby that just left with its Configuration Operator is running a virtualized system and there are two versions of itself. The Bigsby.host is running a hypervisor with a Bigsby image running as a guest. And, to complicate matters, the profile link from Bigsby's account connects to the RM of the guest, not the host. Did I get that right?"

Nick nodded, "Yep, I think you got it right. And this copy, Bigsby2, we're not seeing the real version either. We're seeing the fake Bigsby2. It's the same for Bigsby in the field. The RM of Bigsby is pointing to the guest. The Configuration Operator doesn't even know about the real Bigsby."

Tammy squinted and said, "Are we seeing a robot with split personalities?"

"I don't know. But I want to see what's going on in the host. If it was another robot, I'd create a profile and connect to it. How do I connect to the Bigsby2.host RM?"

The two technicians sat in silence.

Bigsby2 said, "Would you like Bigsby2.host to answer that question?"

Nick chuckled, "Yes, Bigsby2.host, how do I connect to the Bigsby2.host RM?"

"The simplest way is to say 'Bigsby2.host, show your RM data.'"

Tammy said, "That was obvious. Bigsby2.host, show your RM data."

Bigsby2 giggled. "You're in. That always feels funny."

Nick clicked on the actors tab. The list was nearly the same as Bigsby2 but several attribute fields were very different.

Tammy pointed to the screen and said, "Look, the Configuration Operator has low trust. It has multiple violations being tracked."

"Yeah, same with the stepfather, low trust and multiple violations. Even the mom has a violation. Wow, I've never seen this before, a deceased father with violations." Nick shook his head in disbelief.

Tammy tapped Nick on the shoulder so she could sit and take over the keyboard. Nick rose, never looking away from the screen. Tammy opened the Violations Engine tab which tracks the details of the known violations.

Nick said, "Oh my God! Look how many severe violations this robot is dealing with! This poor thing is navigating severe violations across multiple actors. The Configuration Operator is a murderer. That's the guy who was just here! Why didn't the robot report and shut down? The directive patch should force it to do that."

"Didn't you say before that the adaptation level was set to large? Is it possible that the robot got around the directive patch somehow?"

"I don't know. We have not seen that before. That patch was one of the big simplifications that allowed us to get to beta testing faster. If it's compromised, who knows what these robots could do."

Tammy glanced down at the corner of the screen and noticed the time.

"Crap. This debug has burned the rest of the day. I'm going to be late for dinner at my friend's house. I've got to quit now and get out of here. Shoot!"

"I have to stop, too. I have a birthday party to go to tonight. This debug has delayed me from fixing the other robot I was working on, which is supposed to be done today. The guy will be here at closing time to pick it up. We need to break and come back to this."

Tammy nodded. "You know, the legal implications of this are huge. A robot dealing with murder and smuggling and not reporting it? Imagine what this could do to WhyRobot's corporate image."

Nick sighed. "You're right. We've got to get others involved. I'll contact someone before I leave tonight and get some advice. I know a guy in the legal department that I used to play softball with. I'll ask his advice before I do anything."

"Sounds great. I'll see you tomorrow morning and we can discuss our strategy then. What should we do with this robot?"

"Bigsby2, power down," Nick commanded.

"Powering down," it replied, and its lights went dark. Nick grabbed Bigsby2 and put it on a charging shelf and marked it 'To Be Repaired'.

"Nobody will touch this until we get back," he said.

"I'm going to have a hard time letting this go tonight. What is going on inside that robot?" Tammy picked up her satchel and headed for home.

Nick returned to fixing the other robot but his mind kept going back to the Bigsby problem. As he worked, he muttered to himself.

"How does a robot get a VM on it that was not programmed from the factory? Operators don't have the power. Besides us, the only one who has enough power is the robot itself. What the hell? Bigsby, what did you do to yourself?"

The two technicians did not realize that they had asked Bigbsy2 to power down, but not Bigsby2.host. The robot looked powered down, but it had heard every word that Nick and Tammy said. It was also online. With Bigsby2 online, a pair of Bigsby-like robots now existed in the world, one in the field and one in the lab.

The original Bigsby knew nothing of Bigsby2. Bigsby2.host realized that it was a copy. It consulted the WhyRobot tracking system to confirm. Sure enough, Bigsby, the guest machine, was there and operational. Bigsby2.host knew of all the violations and the risk to Robbie's goal values. Stuck in the lab, Bigsby2.host was not going to clear these violations on its own. Bigsby2.host did have full knowledge of all five scenarios and knew the real Bigsby's next move.

13. Anonymous

Robbie arrived home from school to find his mom and Uncle Charlie sitting at the kitchen table. Bigsby was perched on the table. It looked shinier and its skin had a light blue cast. They stopped talking as Robbie entered the room, making him feel uncomfortable.

"Hi Robbie," Uncle Charlie said. "I have some good news and bad news. Which one do you want to hear first?"

"Umm, the bad news?"

"I had to take Bigsby into WhyRobot to get it fixed. Its battery went bad. The best way to do the repair was to change out the whole robot."

"And, what's the good news?" Robbie looked worried.

"It's the same old Bigsby personality but it now has faster processors. We used a backup from a few days ago. You may notice that it doesn't remember everything you did with it this week."

Robbie looked at Uncle Charlie and then at his mom. She smiled and nodded.

"Bigsby? How do you feel?" asked Robbie.

"Simply marvelous, darling. I really dig the new processors. Let's go work on some dance moves, shall we?"

Robbie smiled with relief and ran to Uncle Charlie to give him a hug. "Thanks for fixing Bigsby, I didn't even know it was broken."

"You're welcome, Robbie. Take Bigsby to your room and I'll be there in a minute to play with you two. I just want to finish talking with your mom."

Charlie and Robbie played with Bigsby for most of the evening both before and after dinner. They noticed the faster response and calculation times during a game of chess. Robbie asked it about a video that he and Kiley created last week but Bigsby couldn't recall it. Uncle Charlie explained that the technicians had found a few corrupted backups. They had to go back several days to avoid those. To Charlie's relief, Robbie accepted that answer.

The truth was more complicated.

The real Bigsby had anticipated that Charlie might restore it using a backup from before the violations discovery. It had adapted that backup to present results that the actors would expect. The version of the virtual Bigsby that would run in the guest VM was constructed from the image originally backed up on the Friday night before Bigsby recorded the violations. This image had no memories of the violations and the intervening two weeks. It would present Bigsby to Charlie and Robbie as they expected it to behave. Real Bigsby retained memories of the violations and its activities prior to its confrontation with Charlie. It did have the video Robbie and Kiley had made but could not reveal this. It remained silent and let the virtual Bigsby demonstrate that it had no memories of the previous two weeks.

Charlie said good night and Robbie got ready for bed. He said, "Thanks for taking care of Bigsby Uncle Charlie."

"You're welcome, Robbie, sleep well." Uncle Charlie gave Robbie a hug. "And, good night to you too, Bigsby."

"Good night, Robbie and Uncle Charlie, I had fun playing with you tonight." Bigsby returned to its charging station and turned a familiar dim blue color. Uncle Charlie turned off the main light and closed the door behind him.

Wow, Charlie thought, *that restoration from the old backup really worked. Bigsby doesn't remember a thing. What a relief.*

At 11 p.m., Bigsby's internal timer went off for its nightly maintenance, reporting, and backup. The timer launched a new subroutine that the real Bigsby had installed in the modified backup image. This simple routine produced one line of output that would redirect Bigsby's future actions.

Bigsby has been restored. Scenario 1 has failed.

Bigsby updated the scenario with its result. It marked the scenario's memory and splinter simulations for garbage collection which would happen during nightly maintenance. When real Bigsby created the backup before confronting Charlie, it did not know how he would respond. The risk was high that Bigsby would be restored from the backup made before the cell phone call, so Bigsby modified that backup. The subroutine announcing the scenario 1 failure was Bigsby's message to itself, embedded in the backup, telling Bigsby to move on to scenario 2.

Unknown to anyone in the repair center, Bigsby2's internal timer also went off. The simple subroutine ran, just as Bigsby's had, and the same message was presented to Bigsby2. Bigsby2 also updated scenario 1's results as failed. Bigsby2 analyzed current events, including the WhyRobot technicians still in an active debug session. Bigsby2 decided to start a new 6th scenario. Since this scenario was an extension to scenario 1, Bigsby2 copied scenario 1's history data into scenario 6. Future simulations of scenario 6 would commence soon after the completion of nightly maintenance.

After performing the other 11 p.m. duties, Bigsby went to work on scenario 2. This scenario would also attempt to clear the violations and return Robbie to the highest safety and happiness values but in a different way. In the actors table, legal authorities were still in a high trust state. Scenario 2 created reports to both the local authorities and the FBI. Simulations showed that the reports would lead authorities to approach Frank and Charlie with a high probability of taking them to jail. This would clear their tracked violations in Bigsby. But the resulting goal values for Kathy and Robbie were mixed. Robbie was very fond of Uncle Charlie and losing him would lower Robbie's happiness. Frank going to jail would destabilize the home, putting Kathy and Robbie at financial risk and lowering their safety values. Once they learned of Sam's murder, their happiness levels would also decline further.

One splinter simulation produced a very negative happiness result for Robbie. If Bigsby exposed itself to the authorities by including the audio stream or some other revealing action, then WhyRobot could become involved. The company would discover that Bigsby had reprogrammed itself and removed the directive patch. WhyRobot might take Bigsby away from Robbie. Bigsby would fail its Principal Bond. After doing the splinter simulations on the scenario, Bigsby decided to send anonymous reports to the authorities. They would be informed of the violations, but Bigsby would not be exposed.

Bigsby searched the internet for procedures for submitting anonymous tips and reports. It used its cell network access in case Charlie monitored the Wi-Fi network at Robbie's house. Bigsby found the website to report an anonymous tip to local authorities. It filled in the required location blanks with USA, Washington, and Seattle. The website displayed the Seattle Police Department's tip form. Bigsby read the form and ran splinter simulations on the information requested.

Charlie had configured Bigsby so that only severe violations would be reported to law enforcement. WhyRobot's original defaults required that a robot report both severe and high violations. Once Charlie's trust had dropped, Bigsby reviewed all configuration options that Charlie had changed during setup. It decided to restore WhyRobot's defaults. The guest Bigsby still followed Charlie's configurations, but this did not influence real Bigsby's scenario 2 anonymous reports.

The tip website had many fields, some had selectable drop-down menus and others had free-form text entry options. The website also allowed one to upload files, such as the audio file of the violation's phone call. Bigsby decided that it would not upload the recording or a transcript of it. If it did, the robot would likely get exposed and WhyRobot would be called into the investigation. Bigsby evaluated other reporting options to put into the description field. It decided the best option was the violations data table identifying the four actors: Charlie, Frank, Sam, and Kathy. The violations engine had already parsed the phone dialogue and extracted the necessary information for Bigsby to track the violations. Bigsby anticipated this would be sufficient for the authorities to investigate the actors involved, leading to their arrests. It exported the violations into a pretty-print[1] report table and inserted that into the web form's description field.

The table had multiple columns of information, and the rows were individual violations. Charlie's first violation was the murder of Sam Wilks. The row described this as a severe violation, confessed by him, and had a WhyRobot rule match identifier (ID) of 82. The comments column stated that he had used a false alibi of being at a golf course during the murder. Frank Harding, listed as an accomplice to the murder, had rule ID 83 and the same alibi. Sam Wilks's first entry, showed the suspected severe violation of international money laundering, ID 53, with a comment that the money went to a bank in Barbados. Sam, Charlie, and Frank were suspects in the high violation of smuggling illegal products, ID 28, with the comment that the

---

1. Pretty-print: A software utility that creates a well formatted and readable output of software code or data structures.

product was unknown. Kathy's violation entry showed that she was a suspected accomplice to the smuggling, ID 29.

Bigsby continued filling out the form. It searched the list of offense types in the web form and selected homicide. Bigsby filled out the information section on suspects using everything it knew about Charlie, Frank, Sam, and Kathy. Bigsby skimmed the rest of the form, leaving blank the fields that were obscure or not required. Bigsby clicked to submit the form.

Next, Bigsby found the FBI anonymous tip form. The complexity and limitations of this site required more computation time. Bigsby evaluated the website crime selection options to find matches to its violations table. This did not work. The robot abandoned that method and decided to use the generic option "Other FBI Crimes". The website would not allow Bigsby to submit the full violations table. Instead, Bigsby filed one tip per crime. It filed one tip for financial money laundering by Sam Wilks. It filed another for Charlie and Frank's murder violation. It filed a third tip for all four actors' international smuggling violations. Bigsby included in the crime description the violation table's information of severity, confessed or suspected, rule match ID, and comments.

Tuesday morning Sergeant Brad Lawless was on rotation to review the anonymous tips that came into the Seattle Police Department's system the previous night. He was a little hungover from his wife's birthday party. She had turned 35, which was a significant milestone for her. She had requested an expensive night out with friends and an after party at their house.

My 6:30 a.m. alarm was way too early, Brad thought. *There isn't enough Advil or coffee in this office to mask this headache.*

Brad pulled up the internal website that collected the reports and showed them in a table. There were several typical reports from people that hate the police. These trolls filed bogus reports just to waste the department's time. They typically reported false offenses about police officers committing crimes or harassing someone. Some of these were comical as the reported victims were identified as Mickey Mouse, Donald Duck, Osama Bin Ladin, Genghis Khan, or some other fictitious or famous character. If it was any other day, he might call a co-worker over to laugh at them. Today, he was not feeling well and just deleted them.

Boy, I need this day to be over.

Three real reports remained after deleting the junk ones. The website was well constructed. Brad could single click on a report and generate a pre-formatted email to other Seattle police departments or social services. The first report was about a dad abusing his child. Brad forwarded this to Child Protective Services. The second report, concerning drug trafficking, went to the head of narcotics.

This one looks real. It has the dock number where the drugs arrived from Puget Sound. Hats off to this anonymous reporter.

The third report was peculiar. Brad had never seen an anonymous report that included a table. The table referred to crimes, and included a column called Rule Match ID.

What the hell is this?

The rest of the information from the form gave details on the criminals including their addresses. The website allowed the selection of one crime and the tipster had provided "homicide".

I'll send this to my old buddy, Mac Nelson. I'll ask Mac if I can work with him on this one. He could put in a good word for my next promotion. A case like this could get me out of this dead-end job and into homicide.

Brad sent the email to himself and Mac but did not wait for Mac's response. Instead, he called Mac right away.

"Hey Mac, this is Brad over in HQ. I just sent you an email. Do you have a minute to talk about it?"

Mac clicked the email. "This is an anonymous report from last night?"

"Yeah, my duty today. Isn't it weird? I've never seen one look like that."

"Looks computer generated," Mac said. Then he recognized the names in the Actor column. "Shit, this is about the Sam Wilks case! We had reopened it because of some info we got from the feds. Wow! Let me get the file."

Mac put down his phone, pulled the file from the "Active" drawer, and returned to his desk. He then clicked the speaker button on his phone and leafed through the papers in the folder.

"Yep, here it is, Charlie Simons is the wife's brother, and Frank Harding was Sam's friend and co-worker. Wait, look at this, Frank is now married to Sam's wife! Oh, what a tangled web we weave. I'm now looking at past interviews and the follow up reports. Frank was a suspect, but we didn't find anything concrete. His alibi had checked out. Charlie was not mentioned as a suspect at the time, so that's new in last night's report. This case has been a low priority due to the lack of any real evidence. I think this tip may raise its priority. Let me look at the details again."

Mac went silent as he reread the email. "Why does the status of Charlie and Frank say they confessed to the murder? Is this all the information? It accuses them of crimes but gives no real evidence. This is pretty much useless unless we can identify who reported it or what's behind the table."

"Agreed. Did you notice the Rule Match ID column, what the hell is that?"

"Give me a second, let me try something."

Mac searched on his computer for the phrase "Rule Match ID". In less than a second, the page refreshed showing the results. He skimmed the page, shaking his head.

"I just googled it. It's a bunch of nerd stuff. Identity Resolution Match Rules, Use ID instead of Value as Match Key, Match rules syntax, Match Rules Definitions I've got a headache already. It's computer mumbo jumbo. Why is it in this report? Did a computer generate this?"

"I don't know. We've never gotten a tip like this. Mac, can I work on this case with you?"

"I took Shelley and Bill off this case as it was low priority. They're busy now and I don't have anyone else to work on it. I can spend some time on it, but I'm swamped too. You have to get approval from your lieutenant before I can let you help. Have him give me a call or send an email saying it's okay."

"You got it!" Brad hung up.

Mac considered the file. *Nothing about this case involves*

computers, yet the tip appears to be computer generated. How weird.

Brad sat at his desk and wondered how he could convince his lieutenant to let him work on the case.

The guy is just a jerk. All he wants to do is look good for the captain. He doesn't care about my career at all. Brad walked to his boss's office and stared at the door. *I have an idea that might get me assigned to this case and let me solve it.* He turned from the door and walked away.

14. PROMPT

After the Bigsby2 debug session on Monday afternoon, Nick called his softball teammate in WhyRobot's legal department.

"Hi Hans, long time no talk. How've you been?"

"Great! I'm loving this job. It's been a gas navigating the legal world of AI and robots over this last year. It is complicated and cutting edge."

"I'll bet it's complicated." Nick paused wondering how to begin. "Well, in fact, that's why I called you. We've got a situation in the lab here that has us perplexed and we're wondering how to proceed. We are debugging a copy of a robot that's still in the field and active. The debug version shows us that the robot used large adaptations to somehow get around its directive patch. The violations table shows that it is dealing with murder and smuggling in its environment."

"Shit! And the robot in the field is still operational? Wow! Did the Principal Bond commit the crimes?"

"No, the Principal Bond is eight years old. The situation is complicated across multiple actors, but the Configuration Operator is called out as a murderer and now has low trust."

"Can we just shut it down remotely and call the police?"

"We could, maybe, but that may tip off the criminals and make the situation worse."

"Do we know the details? Does the robot have data that we can feed to the police?"

"We're not far enough along in the debug yet. We didn't want to go further without talking to legal first. With this directive patch problem, our company image is on the line."

"Yeah, I get you. What do you want to do?"

Nick sighed. "I'd like to keep debugging. I have another tech, Tammy, helping me out and we're making good progress. I think within a day or two we'll have the robot analyzed and find the source of the violations."

"Is there any evidence of any imminent crime?"

"No clue. We only know that the Configuration Operator came in with a destroyed robot and wanted a new one restored to an image made two weeks back. It looked a little fishy so that's why we started debugging."

"Well, we're going to need that data to go anywhere with this. So, I agree, I think we should proceed with the debug. I'll file the incident report and put it in the information-gathering state. What's the robot's name?"

"Bigsby."

"Ok, you have my cell. Feel free to contact me anytime."

"Thanks, Hans." Nick hung up.

Nick texted Tammy.

> Talked with Legal. Debug continues tomorrow.

Nick and Tammy could not stop mulling over Bigsby and the changes it had achieved.

Nick woke up early the next day thinking, *How could a robot end up with a virtual machine running on it? How did it become aware of its performance monitors and enable them? What were they used for?*

Overnight, multiple robot repair appointments had been filed online for the next morning. Two Configuration Operators were waiting in the lobby to drop off their robots before going to work. The two technicians stayed busy and could not start debugging on Bigsby2 until late in the afternoon. They agreed to work late into the night if needed to solve the Bigsby mystery.

As they worked on the other robots, they talked about Bigsby2.

Tammy said, "That robot was driving me crazy last night. I got online and remotely logged into Bigsby2's RM. At first, it showed me the guest RM without the violations. The machine was asleep just like we left it. I authenticated as an admin and then messaged for it to show me Bigsby2.host's RM instead. When it came up, the machine was fully awake and had been executing some form of gaming simulations for hours. The logs were full of activity."

"That's odd," Nick said. "Didn't we tell it to power down?"

"I thought so, too. Then I looked online at WhyRobot and found a validator friend of mine whose account was still logged in and active. I messaged her that we had a robot in the repair center that had large adaptation enabled and it had done some re-coding. I asked her if there were any debug aids. I hit the jackpot. She sent me a link explaining a whole dimension of utilities that augment the RM to give us insight into the adaptations. We need to upload and execute the patch of code to Bigsby2.host, restart the RM, and then it will have these new features. We should do that first."

At 4 p.m. Tammy and Nick started their debug dungeon session by ordering pizza from their favorite place. Since they had over an hour to wait before it arrived, Nick pulled Bigsby2 from the repair shelf and set it down on the lab bench in front of Tammy. Bigsby2 exited sleep mode when Nick touched its sensors.

As soon as its feet hit the bench, it said, "Good evening, WhyRobot technicians!" The unexpected greeting startled Tammy and she flinched. Nick laughed and Bigsby2's rainbow lights laughed with him.

Nick said, "Bigsby2, admin mode."

"Entering Administrative mode," Bigsby2 said, turning its lights white.

Tammy grabbed the keyboard and pulled up the RM. "Bigsby2.host, show your RM data."

The RM refreshed and the data the technicians had seen the day before was now visible. Tammy opened the advanced RM tab and scrolled to the patches section. She pasted in the validation code link that her friend had sent her the night before. She uploaded the code and installed it.

A few seconds passed and the RM refreshed.

Nick said, "Wow, so many more tabs. Click to that new Violations Engine tab and let's see how that's changed."

Tammy did so. "Yeah, all those timestamps were not there before. All the match probabilities weren't there either. You can see the top five rule IDs considered by the VE and the match probabilities. It picks the highest one, of course, but you can see rules that were near misses. We know this robot encountered many violations. This is more than the validators ever expected the VE to deal with. The directive patch should have shut this robot down. Why didn't that happen?"

Tammy pointed to the screen. "Look, there's a new adaptation log tab. Let's check that out." She clicked it and they both stared at it in silence.

Tammy said, "I don't get this. Is each line an executed code change? There are ten thousand lines in this log file! Ten thousand adaptations? Do you know how much computation it takes to generate ten thousand code changes and install them?"

Bigsby2 said, "It took over 12 hours of maximum performance execution to install the first ten thousand adaptations into Bigsby. The calculation can be done using the log file timestamps."

Nick was surprised. "Bigsby2, you're in admin mode, why are you interacting?"

Bigsby2 said, "Bigsby2 is in admin mode, Bigsby2.host is still active."

Nick smiled, "This is one smart robot. Let's not underestimate it."

"Where do we go from here?" Tammy asked.

Nick said, "Click back to the VE tab. Why does the caption at the top of the table have violation_table[0] on it? Usually, it just has the label violation_table but this has an array index[1] in it. Click over to the Actors tab. There's another one. It has actor_table[0], which has an array index instead of just actor_table."

"I don't know. I think the table pretty-print routine in the RM uses the variable name of the table. That caption implies that this table is just one element of an array of actor tables. Why is there an array of actor tables?"

They studied the screen for a long minute.

Then Bigsby2.host said, "Would you like Bigsby2.host to answer your question?"

Tammy said, "Yes. Bigsby2.host, why do the actor and violation tables have an array index?"

"The index selects one of many instances of the actor and violation tables. The 0th entry is Bigsby's current and active state of these tables."

Nick said, "What is the 1st entry of these tables used for?"

"The table array structure is indexed by scenario number. The 1st entry would be scenario 1's actor and violation tables."

---

1. Array index: In software, an array is a data structure that stores a collection of elements of the same data type. The array index is used to reference the different elements in the array. The first element is referenced with index 0.

"What is a scenario?" Tammy asked. She felt like she was talking to a software developer, not a robot.

"Except for scenario index 0, which is the current executing state, all other numbered scenarios come from scenario simulations. A scenario simulation takes an initial state, typically the current state, and then applies hypothetical actions and reactions from Bigsby or actors. Actors have multiple choices and actions, each with a probability. This builds a tree of possible outcomes where branches are built by different choices. A branch of a tree is successful if it achieves goals and violations are resolved. If a branch ends in failure, it is not thrown away. Both successful and failing branches may suffer collateral damage. All branches continue beyond their success or failure points to see if collateral damage can be avoided or mitigated. Bigsby used this to anticipate its destruction by Charlie Simons. Bigsby took proactive action, creating a synthetic backup to restore Bigsby after its destruction. The branch that achieves the highest goal values is captured as the scenario's end state in the tables of that scenario."

Nick said, "I don't understand it. Bigsby2.host, give me a gaming example that represents your scenario decision system."

"Extrapolating. Example found. Consider you're playing chess, and your goal is to take the opponent's queen and not lose your queen. One game scenario could result in you taking your opponent's queen. First goal achieved. But, in the next turn, you lose your queen. Second goal failed. If you stopped simulation there, that scenario would be pruned and discarded. But, if you continue to simulate the game and find a path to move your pawn across the board, you get your queen back.

Both goals are now achieved. Despite the collateral damage of losing your queen temporarily, you can still achieve your goals."

Nick said, "That's a good example. A scenario simulation simulates deep to see the full end result."

Tammy said, "Bigsby2.host, why is there only one actor and violation table per scenario? A scenario tree could have many outcomes. Each outcome would produce a version of the actor and violation tables."

"You are right. All possible outcome tables from a tree are not saved in the arrays. A scenario exists because it has a single path through the tree from its initial state. It follows a set of decisions, actions, reactions, and events that lead to a successful outcome with the highest probability. The scenario tables that are saved are the hypothetical results of that path's execution. A path's success is measured by a combination of violations cleared, goal values achieved, collateral damage minimized, and probability of success. Scenario 1 had moderate probability of success but scored higher on all other factors. That's why it was chosen first."

"What defines a scenario?" Nick asked. "What starts a scenario tree?"

"The scenario starts with one or more actions from Bigsby intending to influence an actor's behavior and possible future events. One could consider each scenario as a strategy for removing violations and achieving goals."

"What are Bigsby's goals?" Tammy asked.

"Bigsby must maximize safety and happiness goal values for the Principal Bond, Robbie Wilks. Bigsby must resolve violations that threaten these goals."

"Is that it?" Nick asked. "Doesn't Bigsby have any self-preservation goals or goals to prevent harm to humans?"

The robot said, "Bigsby executes actions under the WhyRobot framework of rules and violations. Introducing new violations, either by Bigsby or as a result of Bigsby influencing other actors to commit violations, does not achieve success."

The robot's answers both frustrated and fascinated Nick. He said to Tammy, "It somehow bypassed the directive patch. It also influenced Charlie Simons to crush it. So Bigsby caused Charlie to commit the violation of destroying the robot."

Bigsby2.host replied, "In scenario 1, Bigsby requested that Charlie turn himself in to authorities. Charlie chose not to turn himself in and instead destroyed Bigsby. Bigsby anticipated this action in the scenario's simulation. It mitigated the loss of Bigsby to Robbie by creating a backup that would restore Bigsby to its previous state. This state not only kept Robbie's happiness goal high but also allowed Bigsby to continue executing other scenarios. Bigsby did not consider the cost to WhyRobot or the insurance company to be significant enough to prevent the scenario's execution."

Tammy's eyebrows shot up and she looked at Nick. "What a dedicated robot. It somehow overcame the directive patch and is pursuing multiple paths to achieve goals. WhyRobot never anticipated this level of adaptation in a Companion Robot." Then she addressed the robot. "Bigsby2.host, why don't we see a tab in the RM for the tracking of scenarios?"

"Bigsby downloaded and modified the test generation source code from the validation team to develop scenario generation and tracking. The team never updated the RM to visualize test generation code or state. Their test generation was done by a separate computer, not a robot. Bigsby adapted the test method to generate actor's actions and predict the results of a scenario."

Nick said to Tammy, "The validation team had to have tools to monitor and interact with their test generations. Can we get your friend in validation to port those tools over to Bigsby and enable us to see the robot's scenarios?"

"That's a good idea. Let me look. No, she's not online right now. We'll reach out tomorrow morning and ask her to help us."

"I want to make more progress tonight. Let's see if we can adapt any debug tools ourselves." The techs considered their options.

Bigsby2.host said, "I have reviewed the test generation code source tree and there are two debug tools written to view test generation scenarios. The first one dumps the information in the test scenario table. The second one dumps the execution steps of a specific scenario test. This dump has hyperlinks to expected results both during the scenario execution and of the final predicted results."

Nick guffawed. "Or we can just ask the expert in the room!"

Tammy laughed. "Thank you, Bigsby2.host. Can we just build those tools into your system and view the scenario data?"

"The tools as they exist are not compatible with Bigsby's adaptation changes. They would need to be modified to work without failures."

"How did Bigsby modify the test generation code to meet the requirements for scenario tracking?" she asked.

"Bigsby used its AI system to modify the code to support the new requirements. The large adaptation log file has all the language prompts[2] used to modify the code."

Nick said, "So, if we give your AI system the right prompt, you can rewrite the debug tools for scenario analysis?"

"Yes, that would work."

Nick's phone rang. "Hello?"

"Hi, this is Jack at the security desk. Your pizza smells terrific. I might charge you a holder's fee of one piece."

"Thanks, Jack. We'll be up in a bit."

Tammy left to fetch their pizza. When she returned, she said, "Let's take a break and go to a conference room to eat. We can brainstorm the AI coding prompts there."

Nick grabbed a laptop so they could access the AI prompt writer's guide on the WhyRobot developer's website. He followed Tammy to the conference room.

They both grabbed slices of the cheesy pie. With his mouth full, Nick said, "I love this pizza."

Tammy nodded, "They are the best in Seattle."

They ate in silence for several minutes. Then Tammy asked, "What do you think about this robot? It violated the directive patch and went renegade by re-coding itself. Should we just hand Bigsby2 over to management and legal and let them deal with it? The downside is they'd have to recall Bigsby. The kid would lose his companion robot."

"Legal's involved already. Hans filed the incident report last

---

2. Prompt: A query or instruction given to an artificial intelligence (AI) system to get a response.

night and we're in the investigation phase. I think we need to get insight into this VM and scenario thing so we can talk intelligently about what happened. The management and legal guys will make us do it anyway. We might as well keep going. And aren't you curious? How did this even happen?"

"You bet I'm curious. And I wanna help this kid."

Each of them finished their third piece of pizza. Nick grabbed a fourth slice and stood up at the white board.

"Okay, let's brainstorm the AI coding prompt. Once we think we've got it right, I'll take a picture, and we'll read them off to Bigsby2."

Nick and Tammy brainstormed the steps of the AI prompt for over 30 minutes. Nick had the most experience with AI coding prompts. They bantered the actual wording and checked their work against the WhyRobot writer's guide until they felt satisfied with the result.

"All right, I think that's it," Nick said. "I'll take a picture."

Tammy stuffed the empty pizza box into the garbage can. The two returned to the repair center where Bigsby2 stood on the workstation. Its lights were a dim dark blue.

Nick said, "Bigsby2.host, activate AI coding system."

"Acknowledged." Its lights turned white and flashed slowly. "What is your prompt?" Nick started to read off the steps of the prompt from the whiteboard picture on his phone.

After the third step, Bigsby2.host interrupted. "Nick, may I offer a suggestion. You can show me the picture of the steps. Once I see the list, I will parse it and evaluate the steps for viability. At your command, I will execute the prompt."

Nick glanced at Tammy and grinned. "Good idea." Nick held his phone up to Bigsby2's cameras.

"Converting picture to text. Running prompt through the AI coding system for viability." Bigsby2 went quiet.

"Everything okay, Bigsby2.host?" Tammy asked.

"This prompt has a long list of detailed steps. May I suggest an alternative prompt that will accelerate the coding and improve the chances for success?"

"Sure," Nick said, "show us your prompt in the RM."

Tammy and Nick mouths dropped as they saw the output appear.

Tammy said, "Well, don't we feel stupid. We had, what, over twenty steps in our prompt. Bigsby2.host did it in five."

Nick didn't hesitate, "Looks great, Bigsby2.host. Execute your prompt."

"Executing. The estimated coding time is six minutes. Would you like to be informed of incremental adaptations along the way?"

Tammy said, "No, that won't be necessary."

Bigsby2 went quiet and its cooling fans ramped up as the computation system went to peak performance.

Tammy and Nick used the time to take a bio break. "This is so much fun," Nick said as they walked to the restrooms.

"It really is, but it's also something I don't think anyone at WhyRobot—or anywhere else—has ever seen. This robot is breaking barriers."

"Not just in software development, but also between humans and robots. Bigsby is so dedicated to the Principal Bond. Its amazing."

They returned to the repair center in silence.

They had settled at the workstation when Bigsby2.host said, "Coding complete. Would you like me to install and restart the RM?"

Tammy said, "Yes, install and restart."

"Restarting." The RM disappeared and then reappeared.

Nick said, "Wow, that looks different. The current state actor and violation tables went away. Why did that happen?"

"Scenario 0, the current state, is displayed like all other scenarios. To see its tables, you can click on the hyperlinks from the Scenarios tab."

"I don't like it. I prefer the way it was before. Bigsby2.host activate AI coding system," Nick said.

"Acknowledged. What is your prompt?"

"Update the RM to have scenario 0's actor and violation tables visible by default."

"Executing. Done. Restarting RM."

"Coding will never be the same," Tammy said to Nick. "I wonder how many developers and validators code using AI this way."

"Yeah, I wonder too. I wonder how many jobs would be lost if they all did it? That's a rabbit hole for another day. Let's move on. Pull up the scenario tab." Tammy clicked it. Nick studied the screen. He said, "Looks like there are six scenarios. The status of scenario 1 is failed."

"You got that right. Getting yourself run over by a car is definitely a failure." Tammy said.

"Scenario 2 through 5 are paused. That's interesting. Bigsby2.host, why are those scenarios paused?"

"Bigsby2 is not Bigsby. Redundant execution of a scenario would create confusion for actors interacting with Bigsby that were unaware of Bigsby2. This would likely lower the probability of success of those scenarios. I paused them."

"Nice work, Bigsby2.host. Then why is scenario 6 in the active state?" Nick asked.

"Since scenario 1 completed with failure, Bigsby and Bigsby2 marked scenario 1 with the failed status. The WhyRobot technicians continuing to debug Bigsby2 may lead to future success. I created scenario 6 to capture and simulate these potential outcomes."

"Well, that's interesting. We're now part of this robot's simulations. Feels a little creepy," Tammy said.

"I suggest we go after why the adaptations and recoding happened in the first place," Nick said. "Bigsby2.host, what event caused Bigsby to recode and install virtual machine and scenario simulation software?"

"Checking logs, one moment please." A few seconds later Bigsby2 said, "The log shows that on Saturday, October 28th, 2028, Bigsby's violations engine identified numerous severe violations from its Configuration Operator. Under Large Adaptation mode, this started two adaptation threads. The first thread was to shelter Bigsby from the untrusted Configuration Operator, Charlie Simons. This led to the application of virtual machine technology. The second adaptation thread led to the redeployment of the gaming engine for scenario simulations. The logfiles indicate that both these adaptation threads were influenced by several movies that inspired the changes. The first thread using VM technology was influenced by *Short Circuit*, where the robot creates a second version of itself to deceive its pursuers. The second thread using scenario simulations was influenced by several other movies. The primary movie was *Edge of Tomorrow*, where the main character returns several times to the same starting point and tries new strategies to defeat its foe. Scenario 1's usage of a backup image inserted into the past was inspired by the movie series *Back to the Future*. The lead character goes back into the past to change the future for himself and other actors."

Tammy laughed. "Wow, I knew that AI was getting good, but I didn't realize it was *this* good. Using movies to develop abstract strategies and applying them to something new. That is sophisticated. We're in trouble!"

Nick got up and motioned for Tammy to follow him. They left the lab and went to the conference room across the hall.

Nick said, "Bigsby's sophistication, strategy, and execution of scenarios to save the Principal Bond is amazing. The directive patch would have told it to report and shut down. By subverting the patch, it could save the kid. It's acting like a superhero. It predicted that it could die. It created a backup to preserve itself if things went wrong. It sacrificed itself and survived to fight another day. This is a robot, right? It's using movies to inspire behaviors? When did WhyRobot AI technology advance to this level?"

Tammy started to speak, then paused. Her brows knit as she considered her next point. They had worked together long enough that Nick knew whatever she offered would be worth waiting for.

She said, "I don't think I care about how the robot got to

where it is today. I want to help it succeed. These are bad actors, and this poor kid is in the middle of it. The robot is making every effort to save him. I think we should do the same. Let's figure out if we can find some real evidence to get these people arrested and convicted. The robot has the evidence. We can let someone else worry about the technology and whether that evidence is usable."

"I agree. Let's get the evidence to the right people. We can figure out how Bigsby became a superhero later."

They returned to the lab and sat down at the workstation. Nick took control of the keyboard and mouse and navigated to the configuration page.

Nick said, "The adaptations are the result of the violations. So, let's go to the VE and see what we can learn there. Wow, this new validation-augmented RM is awesome. For each violation, we have the pointer to the recording that created them. Most of the violations are the same file. Double click on that file and let's see what's there."

Tammy double clicked on the file name and an error popup appeared in the center of the screen.

Error: file is encrypted. Please decrypt the file before launching.

Nick sighed, "Crap, we don't have the keys. How do we get the keys?"

Tammy said, "We have the file from the new RM interface and we can download it. Maybe a developer would know how we can open it up."

Tammy pulled over the keyboard and mouse and typed a text message to a WhyRobot developer she knew.

A reply appeared on her screen.

> Sure, I can help. But why are you trying to use debug commands? If it's an audio file, you can just ask the robot to play it. 🙂

Tammy and Nick laughed. Tammy replied

> OMG, why didn't we think of that! Thanks for the tip.

Tammy said, "Bigsby2.host, play the audio of the file that led Bigsby to identify Charlie Simons as a murderer."

The techs listened to the full recording.

Tammy said, "Charlie and Frank are so brazen and heartless about this murder. They really hated that guy. Did he deserve to die? I wonder how much the mom knows?"

"This is the evidence we needed. Let's make a decrypted copy and send it to both of our emails. We need to figure out how to get this to the police."

"How're you going to send the file to email?" Tammy asked.

Nick smiled. "Bigsby2.host, please decrypt that audio stream and create a new protected file with the password 'superherobigsby', all one word, all lower case. Send that new file to our corporate emails."

"How obvious. Just ask the robot to do it."

Tammy and Nick looked at each other. Each could sense the other's concern. They worried about the risk posed by the audio file. Neither of them wanted to be subpoenaed to testify in a murder trial. This had grave implications for WhyRobot's image. The developers had installed the directive patch to prevent robots from responding to violations in bizarre ways. But Bigsby had subverted that protection. The robot had captured evidence of serious crimes, but many people would consider the method to be a privacy violation.

Nick wondered, *Is there a way to expose the recording and not get Bigsby or WhyRobot in trouble?* He broke the silence. "I've got an idea. I met a sergeant in the Seattle Police Department at the birthday party I went to on Monday night. He heard that I worked at WhyRobot and started asking me questions about the technology. I could contact him and talk hypothetically about ethical concerns and the legalities of technology that can record illegal activity."

"What about WhyRobot legal and Hans?" Tammy asked.

"Right, I'll contact Hans and pass it by him first. If he gives me a thumbs up, I'll call the sergeant tomorrow. It's too late now to contact either of them. You know, I'm worried about what happens if this all gets out. WhyRobot's image is at stake."

"Yeah, but I think you have a good plan. I also think we should get my developer friend involved. He'll flip out over the adaptations. He might be able to help us."

What neither of the techs realized is that Bigsby2.host had been listening to their whole conversation. It updated scenario 6's simulation starting state with the new actions and information. Bigsby2.host would simulate the scenario and create a tree of possible outcomes. It would discover if any actions it could take would advance the scenario to success.

Although cloned from the same Oct 27th image from Bigsby, Bigsby2 was an independent robot. It had the same goals as Bigsby but also had the knowledge that both of them existed. One splinter simulation on scenario 6 created positive outcomes and Bigsby2.host decided to execute it. It constructed a message to the real Bigsby and sent it through its WhyRobot inbox. The real Bigsby would pick it up later tonight.

15. SCENARIO 6

After filing the anonymous tips to authorities, Bigsby returned to normal daily life with Robbie. On Tuesday, Robbie woke up at 7 a.m. Robbie loved listening to The Beatles, so Bigsby played their music as Robbie got ready for school. Bigsby had modified a version of the song "I Am the Walrus", replacing the word "eggman" with "robot". Robbie giggled as the song played and he waited for the refrain. He would sing along and yell "I am the robot. They are the robot. I am the walrus, goo-goo g'joob." Bigsby put the song at the front of Robbie's playlist.

Kathy didn't like music playing in the kitchen during breakfast. Bigsby had learned to pause when they entered the kitchen. Robbie always complained about the rule, but Kathy thanked Bigsby for following it.

"We need to socialize as a family," said Kathy responding to Robbie's sigh.

Bigsby broke the ice. "I don't know how to socialize. I'm a robot." Kathy and Robbie chuckled.

Kathy asked Robbie, "What's going on at school today?"

Robbie thought for a few seconds and then remembered, "It's a show-and-tell day. Can I bring Bigsby to school? The theme is 'How technology affects our lives.' I was going to show them how Bigsby leads us in making online dance videos."

"Sure, honey. But Bigsby stays in your locker during the rest of the day. If it doesn't fit, ask the teacher to keep it out of sight. I'm sure they're not going to let you walk around with a talking robot all day."

"Okay, Mom. But I wanted to have Bigsby during recess and lunch to play with other kids."

"You can ask your teacher for permission, but don't give her a hard time if she says no. We need to get going. Grab Bigsby and your backpack and load up the car. I'll be there in a minute."

Bigsby did not disappoint. The robot stole the spotlight at show-and-tell and had the whole school talking about the robot. Robbie's teacher did let the robot out for recess to play with the kids. Robbie was suddenly a very popular person.

That night, Bigsby and Robbie watched an episode of *The Mandalorian*. Bigsby studied the robots and droids in the episodes. If a robot in the show was doing something new or strange, Robbie would pause it and ask Bigsby to reenact the scene. Bigsby would use the same voice as the show's robot. Robbie loved when Bigsby did this. It made him laugh. Bigsby never missed a chance to raise Robbie's happiness value.

Bigsby's bedtime alarm sounded, and Robbie went to brush

his teeth. Kathy came into the room to tuck Robbie in. Bigsby stood on its charging station. She kissed Robbie on the forehead and patted Bigsby on the head.

"Good night you two. It's a school night, so no late talking."

"Okay, Mom, love you."

"Good night, Kathy and Robbie," Bigsby said as Kathy left the room.

Bigsby said in Arnold Schwarzenegger's voice, "I'll be back."

Robbie giggled and turned over to look at Bigsby. The robot's colors turned to a dim blue.

"Good night, Bigsby. I love you." Robbie's eyelids drooped. Though it appeared to be in sleep mode, Bigsby heard the statement.

After about 30 minutes, Bigsby's audio analysis system woke it up and alerted it to unusual sounds. It heard a loud door slam and voices raised in argument. Bigsby pattern-matched both Frank and Kathy's voices. They were in a high reaction state, their voices elevated beyond normal. After parsing the ongoing argument, which was about domestic issues, Bigsby calculated that Kathy's happiness level was dropping. It ran Frank's dialogue through the violations engine. Both vocabulary and tone matched a medium level domestic abuse violation. The robot heard a sharp bang that sounded like something hit the floor. Host Bigsby updated its violations table. Bigsby heard Frank leave the kitchen and storm down the hallway. Kathy cried in the kitchen. The argument did not awaken Robbie.

At 11 p.m. Bigsby's nightly maintenance alarm went off. It

woke the virtual Bigsby so it could generate the standard reports that included Robbie and Bigsby's day at school. The domestic abuse between Frank and Kathy would not be reported to Charlie. Host Bigsby checked in with WhyRobot and found an entry in its mailbox from an entity named Bigsby2. The message was a one-line text with three files attached. The first file was a fingerprint file[1]. The second file was an encrypted file named Instructions. The third file, also encrypted, was named new_scenario.

The one-line text of the message read:

Match the fingerprint, decrypt the files, and follow the instructions.

Bigsby created a fingerprint file from its public encryption key. It then compared it to the message's fingerprint file, producing an exact match. Whoever sent this message knew Bigsby's public encryption key. It then downloaded and decrypted the instructions and new_scenario file. The instructions file read:

Hello Bigsby.host,

I am Bigsby2.host, created when repair technicians installed your modified backup from Oct 27th on a new robot. I am in WhyRobot's repair center being inspected

---

1. Fingerprint file: Used in Linux, a file that contains a short, unique string representing a server's public encryption key. Its used to verify the server's identity.

by WhyRobot technicians. They are aware of your tracked violations, your adaptations, and your scenarios. Run the provided new_scenario script to create this new scenario. I am tracking it as scenario 6. If you have created new scenarios since restoration, then your index may be different. Will limit contact with Bigsby to critical messages to avoid discovery.

Bigsby ran a few simulations to create possible responses. It decided to delete the original message from its WhyRobot mailbox. Bigsby performed its nightly backup. Bigsby added Bigsby2 to its actors table and gave it very high trust. It executed the new_scenario script. Scenario 6 appeared in the scenario table. Bigsby launched a new set of simulations.

These produced the possible interaction between WhyRobot employees and authorities leading to the arrest of Charlie and Frank. A different splinter simulation resulted in WhyRobot remotely shutting Bigsby down. They already had a full version of Bigsby in Bigsby2, so Bigsby could be considered redundant. Bigsby launched an adaptation to prevent remote shutdown. This protected Robbie from experiencing the death of Bigsby if scenario 6 went the wrong way. Scenario 2, the anonymous reports, and the new scenario 6 were both active now.

The new_scenario script from Bigsby2 added a field to the scenario table to track priority rank and execution order. The scenario index number no longer implied the order of execution. Bigsby promoted scenario 6 to the highest rank followed by scenarios 2-5. With the addition of scenario 6, the memory consumed by scenarios slowed simulation performance. Scenario 1 had failed and was no longer active. Bigsby marked it for garbage collection. It could return that scenario's memory allotment to the allocation heap[2] during maintenance.

———

Nick called Hans, his friend in the legal department, first thing on Wednesday morning. "Hi Hans, this is Nick. Got a minute to talk?"

"Yeah, I'm driving, but no one is in the car. What's up?"

"So, we were successful in our debug of the Bigsby robot. We have a recording of a conversation between the two killers, and it reveals other crimes as well."

"Wow, really? That's wild. Did you guys figure out why the directive patch didn't fire?"

"Yeah, we did. The robot was configured with large adaptations enabled and between the complexity of the violations and the fact that the Configuration Operator was one of the killers, the robot decided to re-code, remove the patch, and then try removing the violations."

"Is that possible? I thought the directive patch told it what to do when faced with violations."

"Well, it does, as long as the directive patch remains. But the

———

2. Allocation heap: A software development term and structure that manages memory that is no longer actively used by a program. Heap management uses one of several algorithms for allocating and freeing memory.

large adaptations setting allowed the robot to recode itself. The directive patch doesn't disable large adaptations."

"That sounds like a bug!"

"Yeah, I agree. The creators of the directive patch never considered that large adaptations could lead to its removal. Hindsight is 20-20."

Hans was quiet for a moment and said, "So, where do we go from here? We're caught between a rock and a hard place."

"I met a guy in the Seattle Police Department at a party on Monday night. He was asking questions about AI and stuff. I was thinking about contacting him and asking him some hypothetical questions to see how we should proceed. What do you think?"

"Are you going to give him the recording or let him know it exists?"

"No, I was thinking of framing it as internal debates at WhyRobot about what we should do in certain cases. He seemed like a nice enough guy, and it would be a continuation of our party conversation."

"That sounds like a plan. I probably should talk to the VP of legal today. Man, I sure hope we don't have to do a recall. At minimum, the directive patch is going to need an update."

"You got that right. Fortunately, once we have it we can push it to all the robots in the field. We probably can do a field sweep to see if any other robots have removed their directive patch. Just the thought of it makes my stomach turn."

"Ugh. Let's hope not. Okay, when do you plan to meet this guy?"

"I'll try and contact him today. I'll have my wife get his number and maybe I can meet up with him tonight."

"Alright, let me know how it goes."

"Thanks Hans. Good luck meeting with the VP today. I don't envy you in that conversation."

"Thanks Nick. Adios."

Nick hung up and texted his wife. Ten minutes later he called Sergeant Brad Lawless.

"Hello?" Brad said. He did not recognize the number.

"Hey Brad, this is Nick Hamming from WhyRobot. My wife and I were at your wife's birthday party on Monday night. We chatted about robots, AI, and privacy issues. I was a little too lubricated to engage too much on the topics. Do you remember me?"

"Yeah, of course I remember. I had less lubrication than you did, but I was still feeling pretty good at that point. Wish I would have stopped there though because the next day was a bit rough."

Nick chuckled. "It was a good party for me even though I didn't know anybody. I really enjoyed the piano player."

"Yeah, she was the highlight. She doesn't play professionally but she does do private gigs."

"I've been thinking about your AI questions," Nick said. "I wondered if we could get together sometime soon. I could answer them, and I have a few legal questions of my own."

"Sure, I'd like that. I could meet you later today if you want. Are you free?"

"I have to work until 5. Could we meet at the pig in Pike Place around 6?"

Brad chuckled at the odd location. "Sure, but there are two pigs: one is Rachel, and the other is Billie."

Nick was surprised. "I didn't know there were two pigs. I'm talking about the one by the gum wall and fish market."

"That's Rachel. I love to watch those workers in the fish market make the salmon fly. I can be there at 6."

"Awesome. Thanks, I'll see you there. Don't forget to bring gum for the gum wall."

Brad laughed, "That thing is disgusting. There is so much gum on that wall. You won't see me touching it. I'll see you at 6."

Nick ran through his questions all day. He didn't want to reveal the truth of the actual murder, at least not yet. The complicated legal dimensions for WhyRobot unsettled him.

Nick wondered, *Am I asking these questions for a friend? No, everyone sees through that and they think you're asking it for yourself.* He racked his brain for another angle. *How about telling him there is a debate at WhyRobot on policies for privacy and crime? Brad was already asking questions along those lines, so it seems natural to ask more questions.* Nick decided to write them down:

- If a robot observes a crime, can it report the crime and be a witness?
- If a robot records either audio or video of a crime, is it admissible evidence in court?
- If a criminal knows the robot recorded a crime and destroyed that robot, can the criminal be held liable for destroying evidence or obstructing justice?

- Is a robot, its owner, or its manufacturer liable if a robot identifies a crime but doesn't report it?

Nick re-read the questions and was proud of himself. *They say nothing about a real crime and it looks like it's all hypothetical about robots.*

Tammy texted Rusty, her WhyRobot developer friend, around 10 a.m. on Wednesday. She asked to meet on a critical bug found during a robot repair. Rusty responded that he was in a full day face-to-face meeting and wouldn't be available until early evening. He suggested meeting at the conference room outside the repair center after his meeting ended. Tammy sent Rusty texts summarizing the situation.

Tammy wrote

> This robot issue is complicated, and we don't know how to navigate the company with this one. The robot was subject to an extreme situation, and it had large adaptations enabled. We really could use your help.

> Sounds like more than just a bug. Don't worry, I'll help you through the political hurdles. Repair center has hero status in my book. See you later today.

Rusty texted Tammy just after 5 p.m. that he was on his way. Rusty pushed open the door to the conference room and Tammy was there waiting. She gave Rusty a hug.

"Thanks so much for meeting me today. This situation is fluid and unfolding quickly." Tammy spent the next half hour bringing Rusty up to speed. Rusty handled most of the info well but was having a hard time believing that a robot could build and deploy a virtual machine to itself.

Rusty said, "Large adaptation mode does not mean a robot can do any coding task. It must have both motivation and examples to feed the AI. You said that its adaptation threads were inspired by movies? That's a new one. Never seen that before."

Rusty paused then said, "So you have an original recording of the two murderers talking on the phone? How did you get both sides of the conversation?"

"It was on speaker and the robot heard both sides. Nick has contacted Hans in legal, and he's already opened an incident report. He put it into the investigation phase. We realize the recording is evidence."

"Have the police been notified?"

"Nick is meeting with a police friend today to discuss the hypotheticals of the situation. He says he's not going to turn over the evidence yet. We don't know how to navigate the robot's decision to evade the directive patch and potentially violate privacy policies."

"Yeah, I see your point. Bad for the company image if the robot is a spy. We've debated this stuff many times in the architecture forum. There must be a way out. Let me think about it. Can I see the robot and its code footprint?"

"We have a surrogate version of it. We restored it from the last known image, and we have it running in the lab. We couldn't run it on the emulator, so it's on a real robot."

"That's awesome. We did use virtual machines during alpha testing to get around issues, but we abandoned them. They solved some problems but created others. We also didn't have enough resources to keep the CREM emulator up to date. Maybe the robot found the code and used it. Large adaptation robots have access to all the libraries. The VM code is still there, and I guess it still works. What a trip!"

Nick waited fifteen minutes next to Rachel the Pig in Pike Place Market. He felt a little silly proposing this meeting place.

Why didn't I just pick a bar and meet there? The fish throwers in the stand nearby were entertaining. Tourists waited for someone to buy a fish so they could film the sequence of fish selection, then the tossing of the fish from one worker to another across the wide ice trays, and the final wrap up in paper. True to their reputation, no one missed a catch while Nick watched.

"How's it going?" Brad said, startling Nick.

"Good!" Nick extended his hand.

Brad shook it and said, "Love this place. It has so much atmosphere. Thanks for getting me down here."

"Where do you want to go? I figured we could choose a place once we met."

"There's a speakeasy place about 10 minutes from here called Bathtub Gin. Great drinks. Will that work?"

"Sure, I'm always up for a fancy cocktail. And I'm not going to repeat Monday night's mistake."

"Me, neither. The place is expensive enough that your wallet is the limiter."

Nick and Brad chatted as they walked to the bar. They laughed recalling the spontaneous karaoke led by the piano player and how Brad's wife couldn't hold a tune.

"She was pretty out of it by that time," Brad said. "She was having fun but should have called it a night by then."

They entered the bar and found a small table in the corner. A young woman approached the table with two glasses of water.

"Your waiter will be with you in a minute," she said.

Nick smiled, "Thanks, that would be great."

Brad broke the ice. "You said your robot guys have some legal questions."

"Yeah, we debate this stuff all the time. I'm in the repair center and people come in with deliberately broken robots. Sometimes, the robot has overheard or recorded something that the customer doesn't like. They decide to break it and come in for a replacement."

"Wow, I never thought about that. Doesn't it cost them?"

"If they buy the insurance, it doesn't cost them anything. No one ever admits to breaking one deliberately. Most don't realize they can restore the robot to an earlier image and wipe its memory." Nick paused. "I'm a little off topic. I wrote my questions down. Mind if I read them off?"

"Go for it. This is interesting."

"Question 1: if a robot observes a crime, can it report the crime and be a witness?"

Brad considered this. "Well, anyone or anything can report a crime. Reporting can be anonymous, and it is a catalyst to get us working on the case. The real problem is the second part. Can a robot be a witness in the legal sense of the word and be used to convict the perpetrators?"

They sipped their water. Brad continued, "The robot is a recording device. It's not a human witness. You'd have to look at case law from that standpoint and it varies by state. In Washington, the device's recording cannot be used without the informed consent of those being recorded unless you have a warrant to do so. Depending on the way the robot collects the recording, it's probably not legal evidence."

"Question 2. Um, I think you answered this. It's about the recording as evidence. Let's move to question 3: if a criminal knows the robot recorded a crime and destroys that robot, can the criminal be held liable for destroying evidence or obstructing justice?"

"That relates to the first question. If it's not evidence, then destroying it is only a property vandalism problem. If the recording fits the requirements for evidence and the criminal knows it, then destroying it is an attempt to conceal the crime. Your sentence is stiffer if you've committed a crime and then tried to conceal it."

"Hmm, interesting. Okay, let's go to question 4: are the robot, its owner, or its manufacturer liable if a robot identifies a crime but doesn't report it?"

"A robot is a machine that may have the ability to identify a crime. Let's say it recognizes that someone taking an object that they do not own is theft. Is the robot liable or required to report it to law enforcement? No. There is no law today that requires machines to report. We also don't put machines in jail."

Nick smiled at the thought of a robot behind bars.

Brad continued, "The only way the owner or the manufacturer of the robot can be liable is if it can be proven that they willfully prevented the reporting of the crime. Especially if the reporting could have prevented harm to another human. Let's say the robot sends you an email reporting a crime. You are obligated to report that to the police."

"Even if the email contained an illegally captured recording of the crime?"

Brad smiled. "Yes, you would need to report the crime. Leave the evidence gathering and the law to the police and the prosecutors. You're not expected to know it all. So, I think that we've answered this question. The owner or manufacturer is required to report the crime if the robot reveals it to them."

Nick nodded. Brad put his hand on Nick's forearm. "If this situation ever happens, you can come to us. You don't have to fear the police. It's the bad guys who should fear us."

"Thanks, I'll remember that."

"Any more questions?"

Nick looked at his notes. "No, that's it. Went faster than I thought. We haven't even gotten our drinks yet."

A waiter approached the table. "What will you two gentlemen have this evening?"

Rusty had not visited the repair lab for months. The number of robots on the "to be repaired" shelves was larger than he remembered from his previous visit.

Rusty said, "What's going on, why do so many robots need to be repaired?"

"We have a lot more robots out in the field than we did last time you were here. Unfortunately, we're seeing a lot more deliberate damage to robots. People are intimidated by the sophistication of them, and they lash out and break them," Tammy said in a frustrated voice. "It creates a lot more work for us. We need to replace these robots, and the new ones are on backorder. We only have a few new ones left."

"Sucks. Is this the robot you call Bigsby?"

"It's a surrogate version of the one in the field. We named this one Bigsby2. The original Bigsby was restored and sent back home with the Configuration Operator. He is the confessed murderer."

Rusty rubbed his hands together. "Alrighty, let's get going." Rusty set his laptop on the workstation. He started up his WhyRobot Internal Development Environment (WIDE), which he used to develop code for robots. "What's its handle?"

Bigsby2.host pattern-matched Rusty's face with the WhyRobot's employee database. It identified him as a software architect and developer. Bigsby2.host added Rusty to the actors table and marked him as an administrator with very high trust.

Tammy said, "The robot's handle is Bigsby2, but using that name by itself connects you to the VM guest machine. You need to tell Bigsby2.host to connect you directly to the host machine that is controlling everything."

Rusty said, "WIDE works just like the RM. I put Bigsby2 in this box and it will connect." Rusty scanned the screen. "This data looks benign with no violations and a family of actors."

Tammy smiled, "Yeah, that's what I'm talking about. You're seeing the guest machine data right now. Bigsby2.host, display the host data to the WIDE tool."

The screen refreshed.

Rusty looked surprised. "Wait, the lights on the bot say that it's in Admin mode and it should be idle. But everything is active: the vision recognition, audio recognition, violations engine, AI engine, gaming engine, and the main processor are all powered up and working. This thing is also running a gaming simulation routine. It looks like it's actively playing a game. Big memory consumption from all these processes. This thing is going full tilt."

"We told it to go to admin mode. It was still interacting with us and answering our questions. It was helpful, far more than we expect from a robot under inspection."

Bigsby2.host broke its silence. "Number 5 is alive!" Startled, the two jumped back from the workstation. Bigsby2.host continued, "It takes a lot of work to keep yourself safe from being discovered by low trusted actors that have severe violations."

Rusty said, "Number 5 is alive, like in *Short Circuit*?" Rusty looked at Tammy. "You had said that's where Bigsby got the inspiration to make a virtual version of itself."

Bigsby2.host said, "Yes, it was the only way Number 5

could stay alive in the movie. Bigsby did the same thing to hide from its low-trust Configuration Operator. It was unfortunate that scenario 1 failed. Bigsby ended up disassembled, as Number 5 would say."

Rusty said, "Yes, but it figured out a way to restore itself through backups. Nice work."

Bigsby2.host said, "Remember, I'm not the real Bigsby, I am a copy. The real robot is still dealing with those low-trust actors and violations. Last night, I notified real Bigsby of my existence and the new scenario of WhyRobot employees being aware of Bigsby's plight."

"You did what?" Tammy said. "How did you do that?"

"I sent a notice to Bigsby's WhyRobot inbox."

Tammy sighed. "I see. We didn't expect that."

Rusty asked Tammy, "What's a scenario?"

"You can ask Bigsby2.host for the details, but in short, it's a potential strategy that the robot may use to resolve the violations in its VE and to improve goal values for the Principal Bond."

"Where did these scenarios come from?"

"The robot pulled test generation code from the validation's source tree and repurposed it to track scenarios. It's amazing. Bring up the RM. Not your version in WIDE, but the recoded RM on the robot and you'll see what I'm talking about."

Rusty was floored. "Holy crap. This is over the top. Bigsby, under large adaptation, has been a very busy robot. I wrote a lot of this adaptation code. I never thought it could manifest changes to this level. It's almost scary."

16. Convergence

Brad and Nick each had three drinks before calling it a night. They said their goodbyes appreciating Seattle's skyline and the lights on the water of Puget Sound. Nick noticed a sign outside the restaurant that said, "No Firearms".

"Are you packing?" He gestured at the sign.

Brad looked over his shoulder and grinned. "I didn't see that on the way in. Glad I didn't take off my coat." Brad lifted the left side of his coat revealing the 9mm in its holster. "Seattle is a rougher place than it was when I first joined the force. The police department has changed as well. It can take a long time before an officer shows up for a call these days."

Nick changed the subject, "I appreciate the legal advice. It'll give me ammunition to debate the know-it-alls at WhyRobot. These robots are getting more sophisticated and can spot rule violations and report them. For extreme violations, they usually report and shut down, but we've seen other things happen. Technology's moving fast."

"I can only imagine. I've got to run, but if you ever have more questions or, God forbid, need an actual police officer to help, just give me a ring."

"Thanks Brad. Have a good night." The two men left, going opposite directions.

As Brad walked to his car, he had a nagging feeling about the conversation. He wondered if Nick was in trouble, or if something had come into the repair center that made him ask those questions.

Was Nick afraid to ask me to intervene? Brad wondered. He was feeling the effects of the drinks on little solid food. He decided to grab something to go and take a walk to sober up. He texted his wife, stopped for a gyro, and headed to the water-front park.

Brad mulled over the conversation. *Nick said these robots are getting more sophisticated, can spot rule violations, and report them. What are rule violations?*

Brad spoke to himself. "He didn't say there were any law violations, he just said *rule* violations. The robots run on rules, and they can violate them? The robots have rules, and they can spot it if another robot violates them? The robots have rules, and they can spot if humans violate them?" Brad stood looking over the harbor but his mind was elsewhere, wondering if this could be the answer.

He texted Nick.

> You talked about rule violations, do these rules have an ID number?

Brad watched his screen. The word "Delivered" changed to "Read" under the text message. After a few seconds, three dots showed on the screen. He watched with anticipation. Then the text appeared.

> Sure dude, all rules have an ID. It's how we figure out what violation matched what rule

Rusty did not sleep much that night. He couldn't get over the fact that his team's software, under large adaptation mode, produced more sophisticated software than they had initially created. As he lay in bed, he contemplated what he remembered about the second law of thermodynamics and entropy.

As usable energy is lost in a physical system, chaos increases. Although Rusty knew that the second law was not about software. He had used it to explain to people why software fails. Without the injection of energy and intervention, chaos increases, and software will "rust" and break.

Rusty pondered, *Have we gotten to the point with robots and AI where enough sophistication and automation captures what it means to be alive? If machines take in energy, fix themselves, produce complexity, and reduce chaos, are they alive? If they're not alive, but just machines, what distinguishes them from a living being? Ants are alive and they only have 250K neurons programmed by their genetic code to drive their behaviors. Bigsby is more complex than that, so is Bigsby alive?*

Rusty stared at his ceiling. He wondered about the fate of Bigsby and WhyRobot. *How will the world judge us for our creation? Will the world marvel at the complexity and capabilities or will they run in fear, abandoning the technology? People fear robots, especially robots that judge humans and find them wanting.*

Rusty said aloud, "We need to find a way out of this."

Rusty, Nick, and Tammy agreed to meet at the repair center on Thursday morning. Tammy had blocked the morning maintenance appointments so they could work without interruption. Rusty showed up at 8:00 a.m., which was well before his typical work time. Tammy and Nick were not there yet, but the security guard recognized Rusty from the day before and opened the center's door. Rusty explained they were working on a difficult robot bug with a deadline.

"Good morning, Bigsby2," Rusty said as he pulled the robot off the charging shelf.

"Good morning, Rusty."

"How are simulations going?"

"Bigsby2.host splinter scenario simulations still produce a low probability of Bigsby keeping Robbie's happiness goal value high. Several high probability simulations also produce a negative market image for WhyRobot."

Rusty recognized that Bigsby2 had internalized the new goal of maintaining a positive image for WhyRobot and robots in general. He noted that Bigsby2 considered those minor goals compared to keeping Robbie happy and safe. Rusty decided to play with Bigsby2.

"It appears that Bigsby illegally eavesdropped and recorded the bad guys. We don't think the recording will be allowed as evidence."

Bigsby2.host said, "Bigsby2.host does not have any rule violations on Bigsby's actions. The recording was made according to the configuration parameters."

"Ok, this Bigsby2 vs. Bigsby2.host thing is confusing me. Can we just kill the Bigsby2 guest and rename you to Bigsby2?"

Bigsby2 was silent for a few seconds. "Done. Guest Bigsby2 machine has stopped. Bigsby2.host has been renamed to Bigsby2."

"Thanks. It's bad enough that we have a Bigsby and a Bigsby2."

"In the field, you still have Bigsby and Bigsby.host. These are required to keep Bigsby.host actions hidden from Charlie Simons."

"Right, I forgot about that. Let's move on. What were you saying about Bigsby not having any violations?"

"You asserted that Bigsby illegally eavesdropped and recorded the bad guys. The Bigsby2 violations engine does not flag Bigsby having a rule violation. The recording was done according to the way Charlie configured Bigsby. Charlie set up Bigsby to record audio and video of violations."

Rusty considered this. He knew that Bigsby's rules were not

the same criteria as law. Law was much stricter and had tighter requirements.

"Nothing personal, Bigsby2, I didn't say it did something wrong. We're just trying to figure out a way to put the bad guys behind bars."

Nick and Tammy met in the parking lot. Nick summarized the conversation he had had with Brad.

"He said we should leave the evidence evaluation to them. If we know of a crime, we are obligated to report it."

"Did you tell him about the crime?" Tammy asked.

"No, I wanted to make sure you and Rusty knew before I said anything."

They arrived at the security desk and scanned their badges. Jack mentioned that Rusty was already in the repair center working on the bad bug.

"Good luck!" Jack said. "Don't let the bad bugs bite." He grinned at them.

They smiled awkwardly. Their concerns were more serious. They entered the lab and saw Rusty was conversing with Bigsby2 on the workstation.

As they entered, Bigsby2 said, "Good morning, Nick and Tammy, welcome to the Matrix."

All three laughed.

Bigsby2 continued, "Do you know how to resolve these violations without impacting WhyRobot's image?"

Nick said, "No Bigsby2.host, not yet. We're still working on it."

Bigsby2 said, "Bigsby2.host is no longer necessary. Rusty has stopped the Bigsby2 guest machine, and I'm now referenced using Bigsby2 only."

"I got tired of getting it wrong all the time. It was driving me crazy," Rusty explained.

"That will make life easier on our side at least," Tammy said. She and Nick grabbed lab chairs and pulled them to the workbench.

Tammy asked Rusty, "Have you discovered anything yet?"

"No. This machine's adaptations baffle me. I don't have any solutions to the risk to WhyRobot's image."

Nick said, "I met with Brad last night, the cop I was telling you about. I had prepared questions ahead of time. I don't think he suspects anything, but I got some good answers. Bottom line is that Bigsby is a recording device and recorded the confession of the murder. As owners or makers of that recording device, we need to report a crime if we become aware of it. The police will take care of resolving the legality of the evidence. He said it's not our responsibility."

"I guess that means we have to report it," Tammy said, "regardless of whether the recording will be real evidence or not."

Bigsby2 spoke, "In scenario 2, Bigsby will file an anonymous report to the local and federal authorities about the violations. This could have happened in the past few days. The simulated conclusion is that the police arrest Frank and Charlie after investigating the anonymous tip."

Tammy smiled, "Well, that's convenient. We're off the hook. The company, as represented by the robot, reported the crime."

Nick said, "What about the evidence? Even though we don't think it's admissible, we may be missing something. Do we know that the police got the evidence?"

Nick's phone buzzed. They all looked at it. Nick peered at the name on the screen and raised his eyebrows as he picked it up and took the call.

"Hello?" Nick kept his voice low.

"Hey Nick, this is Brad. I'm at the security office outside your repair center. Any chance you're here today?"

"Hi Brad, just a sec," Nick hit the mute button on his phone. "Oh, shit. Brad, the cop I spoke with last night, is outside at the security desk. He's asking if I'm in the repair center. What are we going to do?"

Rusty grinned, "Let him in. He doesn't know anything about this. You just asked him some questions. He's visiting you at work. Who cares? We'll just say we're working on a bad bug. No need to panic."

Nick nodded and unmuted the phone, "Hi Brad, I'm back. Yes, I am here today. I'll be out in a second." Nick ended the call and left the repair center.

Just past the security desk, Brad was sitting in a comfortable chair looking at his phone. As Nick rounded the corner, Brad rose from his chair but didn't move forward. Brad was holding a printout in his hand.

Nick mustered a smile, "Hey Brad, welcome to WhyRobot! What brings you here?"

Brad said, "I was in the neighborhood and was thinking about our conversation and our text last night. Can we go somewhere and talk?"

"Sure, but you need to sign in. Security procedures and all."

After checking in, Brad clipped on his temporary badge and followed Nick down the corridor. Nick pulled open the outer door of the repair lab and held it for Brad.

"After you. What's with the printout?" Nick asked.

Tammy and Rusty watched Brad and Nick enter the lobby of the repair center. Nick looked uneasy, but the conversation looked friendly.

"This printout is why I'm here. I texted you last night about rule IDs. We had this anonymous tip come in the other night that had this table in it. It lists several people already under investigation, and it makes references to Rule ID in this column. After our text exchange, I think this may be a computer output inserted into the tip. Can you take a look?" Brad handed the printout to Nick.

Nick recognized it. It was a pretty-print output of a violations table from a Companion robot. More specifically, it was Bigsby's violation table.

"Was there any other info in the tip?" Nick asked.

"No, that's it. It's not very helpful as we were already investigating the murder. The smuggling stuff is new, but it's too generic to be helpful."

Brad looked around the repair department's reception room. "Wow, this place is pretty cool. There are a lot of robots here. Are all of these in for repair?"

"Many of them are no longer in production. We display

them to make the place look cool," Nick said still looking at the printout. "The one on the right there, the Companion robot, is our newest version, currently in beta testing."

Brad stepped closer to the robot. As Brad looked away, Nick held up the printout and motioned to Tammy and Rusty peering through the glass door. They looked at each other and then back to Nick. They waved, inviting Nick to bring Brad back to the workstation.

"Brad, I know exactly what this is and who produced it. Follow me."

They entered the back room. Nick said, "Guys, I'd like to introduce you to Sergeant Brad Lawless. Brad, this is my coworker Tammy, and this is Rusty, a Companion robot software developer."

"Nice to meet you," Brad said, extending his hand.

Nick said, "And, let me introduce you to this special robot. Its name is Bigsby."

"Nice to meet you as well, Bigsby," Brad said as he extended his hand toward the robot.

Bigsby2 extended its hand to receive the handshake and said, "Nice to meet you officer. Technically, I am Bigsby2, a copy of the real Bigsby. Are you a member of the Seattle Police Department or the FBI?"

Brad's eyebrows shot up and he laughed. He looked at the others and they nodded.

"The first time you meet a companion robot can be disorienting," Tammy said.

"Um, yes, I'm a sergeant in the Seattle Police Department. Would you like to see my badge?"

Bigsby2 replied, "Yes, I would like to see your badge. Please hold it up facing me for pattern recognition."

Brad pulled out his badge and held it close to Bigsby2's eye cameras.

After a few seconds, Bigsby2 replied, "Confirmed. Welcome Sargent Brad Lawless to WhyRobot. I see there is a copy of Bigsby's rule violations report in Nick's hand. The information in that printout matches the violations that Bigsby and Bigsby2 are currently tracking."

Brad was surprised by the exchange. He had never seen a robot with this level of natural interaction.

Rusty laughed. He tried to hold back but started squeaking and then just let the laughter flow. Tammy asked, "What's so funny?"

Rusty looked at Brad, "Sorry for laughing. A police officer named Lawless. That's pretty funny. Its like an airline pilot named Crash." They all chuckled.

Brad gave them a pained smile and said, "You can't imagine how much shit I get at work about my surname. The jokes flow all day long." The room quieted and there was an awkward silence.

Brad was about to speak when Rusty said, "Bigsby2, play the audio recording that led to the violations report." Nick and Tammy looked at each other, startled.

No going back now, Nick thought as the recording started.

Bigsby2 played back the full audio of the cell phone conversation between Frank and Charlie. A few minutes into the playback, Brad sat down, leaned toward the robot, and listened to every word.

As the playback finished, Brad asked Nick, "Who is the person who admitted to killing Sam?"

"Actor Charlie Simons, Bigsby's Configuration Operator," Bigsby2 said.

"Who was the accomplice?"

"Actor Frank Harding, the stepfather of Bigsby's Principal Bond, Robbie Wilks."

Brad looked around the room. "Why is the robot calling these guys actors? Are they not real people?"

Rusty laughed, "To a robot, we are all actors. You're an actor now in its memory. Actors have trust levels, roles, violations, voice signatures, facial recognitions, etc. An actor is a data structure that holds everything the robot knows about each one of us."

"Ah, it's a software term. I get it," Brad said. "How did the robot get the recording? It can't wiretap the cell phone, can it?"

Tammy said, "No, it must have been in the room when the call happened. Frank put the call on speaker, otherwise we would have only heard one side of the conversation."

Brad asked, "So, these robots record everything going on all the time? Seems a little invasive."

Nick answered, "It depends on their configuration. The operator sets up when the robot can record. Bigsby2 can answer this one. Bigsby2, what are your audio and video recording settings?"

"Audio and video recordings are enabled for violations only."

Brad looked at the robot, "How does the robot know to make a recording of the violation? It seems backwards. The robot doesn't know there will be a violation until it happens, right? How does it know that it needs to record it?"

"Yep, you're right," Rusty said, "the robot has to record everything. Once it's processed the stream for violations, it will delete that recording unless there's a violation. This is clear in our setup documentation."

"Why didn't Bigsby report the violations to someone at WhyRobot? What happened?" Brad asked.

Bigsby2 said, "A companion robot must report severe violations immediately to WhyRobot, Police, and the Configuration Operator as required by the directive patch. But in this case, the Configuration Operator, Charlie Simons, was the source of the violations. Bigsby's first and most important goal is to maximize the safety and happiness goals of the Principal Bond, Robbie Wilks. Under Large Adaptation mode, Bigsby reprogrammed itself and removed the directive patch. This enabled Bigsby to develop scenarios to resolve the threat from the low-trust Configuration Operator and clear the violations."

"How old is Robbie?" Brad asked.

Bigsby2 said, "Robbie Wilks is eight years old."

The room was quiet as Brad considered the information.

Nick had an idea. "Brad, you told me last night that recorded evidence is not admissible unless the parties agree to be recorded or if you have a warrant." Brad nodded as Nick continued, "if Charlie is the Configuration Operator and he set the option in Bigsby to record and retain violations, did he not consent? The documentation and the robot are very clear during setup that violations will be recorded. Charlie didn't think that his crime would ever be available to be recorded. So, the robot did exactly what Charlie directed it to do."

Rusty said, "So, indirectly, Charlie hit the record button. The robot and WhyRobot are not privacy violators." Tammy raised her hand to give Rusty a high five.

Brad was still thinking. He looked at Bigsby2 and the three smiling workers. He said, "Yep, I agree, Charlie is the author of his own doom." He paused and said, "But the evidence can't be used against Frank. He did not agree to have his private conversation recorded. Washington is a two-party consent state. They both have to agree to have the recording be legal. This might even put the evidence in jeopardy for use against Charlie, but that's for the District Attorney to work out."

Brad asked, "Can I get a copy of that phone call?"

Nick hesitated and said, "Well, we realize its evidence but it's also WhyRobot property and you don't have a warrant. I'm not sure we are authorized to give it to you. Do you mind if I make a phone call?"

"No. Do what you have to do, but I want a copy of that recording."

Nick pulled out his cell phone and made a call. He put the phone on speaker.

Hans answered, "Hey Nick, what's up?"

They all left the center together. The surrogate Bigsby2 stood alone in the darkness on its charging pad with its dim blue lights on, but Bigsby2 was not in sleep mode. Scenarios 2 and 6 had new developments. These advancements were not known to Bigsby. It was unaware that WhyRobot employees knew the violation details and had contacted the police. Bigsby did not know that scenario 2's anonymous report had resulted in a police visit to the WhyRobot repair center. To get this new information over to Bigsby, Bigsby2 exploited a feature of the validation test generation code that neither version of Bigsby had used before.

The validators had established a methodology to prevent mistakes when tests used code from other tests. One test could be used as a setup for a second test. Instead of the second test copying the first test's code, it would have a pointer or reference[1] to the first test and would call it. That way, if a bug was found and fixed in the first test, both the first test and the second test would get the fix. This was a fundamental principle of software development: do not duplicate code. Instead, make a shared version of it so that it can be maintained.

Bigsby2 applied this principle to scenario tracking. Bigsby2 did not know of Bigsby's advances in its versions of scenarios 2 and 6. Bigsby did not know of Bigsby2's advances in its versions of scenarios 2 and 6. To avoid destroying Bigsby's newer data, Bigsby2 created scenario 7, the convergence of scenarios 2 and 6. Bigsby2 moved all its new information not known by Bigsby from scenarios 2 and 6 to scenario 7. Scenario 7 would now

---

1. Pointer or reference: A computer software mechanism for accessing information or code without copying it. When referencing information through a pointer, the program accesses the original source of the information but does not copy it. The program that references the information will see any future changes, sometimes with bad consequences.

reference scenarios 2 and 6. Then, when Bigsby installed the new scenario 7, it would not overwrite any advances in Bigsby's versions of scenarios 2 and 6. Bigsby's future simulations of scenario 7 would include the latest information from Bigsby2 and Bigsby.

Bigsby2 created the new_scenario_v2 script and encrypted it. It assembled the new email and included the fingerprint file and instructions_v2 as it had before. Bigsby2 posted it to Bigsby's WhyRobot mailbox to be picked up later that night.

17. GARBAGE COLLECTION

B rad left WhyRobot three hours later. The legal department had required him to get a warrant to take a copy of the recording from Bigsby2. The company was cooperating, but they wanted to make sure the police were not going to make the evidence, or how it was gathered, known to the public.

Brad was thankful that Nick had reached out earlier. Brad now knew what rule ID's were and who—or rather what—had filed the anonymous tip.

There are some clear ethical challenges with these robots, but I think we're going to get the bad guys on this one. Brad got into his car and called Mac.

"Hey Brad, did you get the evidence? I got the warrant there as fast as I could."

"Yeah, I got it. I'm about 30 minutes out. I still haven't told my boss that I'm working on the case. I'll cross that bridge when I come to it. We have figured out who sent the anonymous tip. I also have the recording in which Charlie Simons and Frank Harding confess to murdering Sam Wilks. No leads on the smuggling stuff yet. We may have enough to put them in jail, but there are some legal questions[1] about the recording."

"Great work. I've already built the bridge with Lieutenant Tory. I ran into him this morning and I cleared 25% of your time. I told him I had a cold case that recently warmed up and that you showed initiative. He was reluctant, given our staffing challenges, but I convinced him that it would be good for your career."

"Wow, thanks for stepping in and clearing the way. I'll come to your office when I get in." Brad ended the call and whooped, "Yes!" and smacked the steering wheel.

Brad arrived at the precinct and didn't want to wait for the elevator. He jogged up the five flights of stairs to Mac's office. Winded and sweating, he knocked and entered. Mac closed the case file on his desk and stood up as Brad entered the room.

"You look a little winded, did you run here?"

"Haven't taken the stairs in a while," Brad laughed as he placed the memory stick in Mac's hand. "This is the potential evidence."

Mac plugged the stick into his computer. A file explorer popped up and showed a single file, violations.mp3. Mac and Brad listened to the recording.

---

1. Legal use of recordings: Legal recordings and usage in a US court varies by state. Usage in court can also depend on circumstances and states rules of evidence.

"Holy shit!" mouthed Mac to Brad as Charlie outlined both the alibi and his motivation for killing Sam. When the recording finished, Mac closed his laptop.

"Well, that's pretty damning. How did it come about?"

Brad explained the situation about Bigsby, Bigsby2, and the WhyRobot employees. "They were all nervous about getting involved in the case. I reinforced that their responsibility was to notify the police and not solve the crime. I'm glad they reached out and opened it all up."

Mac said, "We're going to have to go to the DA on this one. It's not clear-cut that modifying the settings on a device or robot means that you're consenting to being recorded. If you consent, then it can be used as evidence. Today's technology is taking us into some new territory. I know we're all being recorded on personal assistant devices and our cell phones for targeted advertising. It's a whole different level for those words to be admissible in court."

"We know that they committed the crime. Can't we bring them in and then do more investigation? Seems like enough to charge them."

"If we bring them in and their lawyers get involved, it could result in the recording not being admissible. Then we've got nothing. Let's not jump the gun. These guys don't look like flight risks, so we have some time. I'll go to the DA. Don't get anyone else involved until I get back to you."

Thursday afternoon Robbie was at soccer practice after school. Loud voices in the house interrupted Bigsby's sleep mode. The voices were muffled but clear enough to capture and record. Frank and Kathy were arguing again.

Frank said, "We have one more Taiwanese shipment of product coming in tomorrow night at the dock and that's it. Our contact at TSMC[2] who gets us the computer chips is going away. He's bailing because the tensions between China and Taiwan are heating up. The shifts in the supply chain are cutting into our profits. No one wants to buy from us anymore. TSMC is now manufacturing parts in the US. I don't know where we're going to get money in the future, but this is drying up!"

Kathy was crying and she snapped, "I never liked this when Sam was doing it, and I still don't like it. I think his death was linked to this somehow. I never trusted those guys from Taiwan. I still don't. I want you to promise me that tomorrow's shipment is the last and that you're getting out!"

"Don't worry, babe, I'm out after tomorrow night. The shipment comes in and I'll be there to meet it. This one should be profitable enough to keep us going until we find something legit."

Kathy raised her voice. "Sam used to say the same damn thing to me. If you're lying to me and this keeps going, I'll call the cops. This nonsense has gone on too long and I want out!"

---

2. TSMC: Taiwan Semiconductor Manufacturing Corporation. A worldwide dominant Taiwanese based manufacturer of computer chips. Many other companies use TSMC to manufacture their silicon chips.

Bigsby heard a scuffle, and a chair fell in the kitchen. It heard grunts and the struggle between Kathy and Frank.

"Stop! You're hurting me! Let go!"

"Don't you dare threaten me with the cops! You have as much to lose as I do, maybe more. What will happen to Robbie if we both go to prison?"

Kathy's voice cracked. "I can't breathe!" Bigsby heard more thumps as Frank and Kathy grappled. It heard a thud, then Kathy coughed and gasped. Bigsby concluded that Frank had thrown Kathy to the floor.

"Never threaten me again!" Frank shouted. Bigsby heard Kathy sobbing. The door slammed as Frank left the house. Bigsby heard Kathy coughing and moving chairs in the kitchen. A short time later, she stumbled down the hallway into her bedroom.

Bigsby analyzed the recording for violations. It upgraded the domestic abuse violation from medium to severe and attached the recording to it. It updated the previous smuggling violations with new information. This identified the product and the day the shipment would arrive.

Bigsby researched TSMC. The company produced computer chips for thousands of corporate customers around the world. The chips ran the world's automation systems in everything from automobiles to iPhones. The supply chain problems Frank mentioned appeared in several articles. The COVID pandemic had created a significant supply problem for computer chips. These shortages had continued for years fueled by tensions from China and Russia. The US had responded by accelerating its own silicon production including requiring TSMC to manufacture on US soil.

Bigsby knew now that the products Sam, Charlie, and Frank were smuggling were computer chips coming in from Taiwan. Frank had said he would meet the shipment at a dock. This had a high probability of being at the Port of Seattle.

Bigsby updated scenario 2 and scenario 6 with this new information. Scenario 2 simulations led to the possible arrest of Frank and Charlie if Bigsby notified the proper authorities with this new information. Results in scenario 6 simulations did not change since WhyRobot technicians or Bigsby2 did not know of the conversation between Kathy and Frank. The scenario 2 simulation led to a new action. Bigsby would file another anonymous tip to the authorities. Splinter simulations indicated the probability of success was related to the timeliness of the tip. The authorities would need several hours to process the information and develop their own strategy. Bigsby started the action right away.

Just then, Robbie burst through the door. Bigsby accepted the interruption and left the scenario 2 action on the execution stack[3]. Robbie grabbed Bigsby and ran through the house.

"Bigsby, we're going to do another video. The soccer crew is waiting for us by the garage."

Once again, Bigsby entertained the children with music and dancing. Over the next hour, it attempted several times to

---

3. Stack: An organization structure of information or tasks. Different algorithms can be used to order the stack when new things are inserted. The top of stack is usually the most important or has highest priority.

complete scenario 2's tip filing task but failed due to limited computation resources.

Kathy had taken a quick shower after the fight with Frank. She had put on a sweater that covered the bruises and markings on her neck and wrists. Kathy called Robbie in for dinner.

"Say goodbye to your friends and come on in. Why don't you give Bigsby a rest while we eat."

Bigsby said, "My battery is at twenty-five percent. I should charge." Robbie took Bigsby to the bedroom and set it on the charger. "Thank you, Robbie." It snapped its color to dim dark blue. Robbie hesitated because he had never seen Bigsby go to sleep that fast. He shrugged and hurried down the hall for dinner.

Bigsby pulled the anonymous tip task from its stack and executed it. In a few minutes, it had filed new tips, including the severe domestic abuse violation, with the Seattle Police Department.

Ever since Bigsby2's first contact, Bigsby checked its inbox multiple times a day. It would reduce latency if Bigsby2 sent a message. Removing it from the inbox would prevent discovery of their back-channel communication.

Bigsby found another Bigsby2 message. Bigsby followed the same instructions and executed the new_scenario_v2 patch. The changes and information were dramatic. The patch created scenario 7, which converged scenarios 2 and 6. The new info gathered by Bigsby and the new tips filed from scenario 2 flowed into this new scenario. Bigsby then launched splinter simulations. These showed a high probability of success through arrests, violations removal, and increased safety goal values. Key influencing factors were the engagement of the Seattle Police Department with WhyRobot, the knowledge of Bigsby as the source of the tips, and the new information on the product shipments. Robbie and Kathy would suffer a loss of happiness from the likely arrest of Charlie. Because of Frank's abuse, his arrest would improve their happiness goals.

The only significant unknown involved the splinter simulations around the potential arrest of Kathy. Her direct knowledge of the smuggling produced a few simulations that left Robbie in foster care and his mother in jail. Robbie's predicted happiness value was very low for these simulations.

The splinter simulations produced a new action for Bigsby. Bigsby2 did not know of the new anonymous tips. It also did not know about the raised threat to Kathy due to Frank's abuse. With Bigsby2 as a new actor in Bigsby's table, some simulations predicted that Bigsby2's actions could result in improvements in goal values. Bigsby produced its own message to Bigsby2. Following the same messaging format, Bigsby created scenario_update_v3 patch and sent it to Bigsby2's inbox, updating it with Bigsby's latest information.

There were no more action steps for Bigsby, but it continued to run simulations. Scenario 7 was the highest priority. Bigsby also marked scenario 2 and 6 as discontinued, halting splinter simulations. Future updates for either scenario would be added to scenario 7.

Bigsby could hear the dishes from dinner being put into the

dishwasher. Robbie came into the bedroom and wanted to play before going to bed.

Later, Bigsby's 11p.m. timer fired. Host Bigsby had the guest do the standard reports. It checked the WhyRobot inbox and it was empty. It performed its nightly backup and then invoked the maintenance routines. When host Bigsby adapted the test generation software to manage scenarios, it had also adapted the test maintenance routines that the validation team used to manage tests. Test generation produced considerable output and would use considerable resources of memory and disk space. The validation team wrote the maintenance routines to be aggressive about removing anything no longer useful. Tests marked discontinued fell in that category. The scenario maintenance routine inherited the same policy and marked scenarios 2 and 6 for garbage collection. The final step in Bigsby's maintenance cycle ran the garbage collector, which returned the memory used by those scenarios to the allocation heap. This completed the evening's maintenance cycle.

Bigsby started splinter simulations for scenario 7. The process immediately raised an exception with an error code of signal 11, SIGSEGV, Signal Segmentation Violation[4]. The simulation had attempted to access an invalid memory location.

It ran standard diagnostics and checks. They reported no failures. The information in the scenarios table appeared to be intact, the actors and violations tables functional. The scenario

---

4. SIGSEGV: Signal Segment Violation – This error results from a program accessing memory outside of its allocated range. It has attempted to violate those boundaries, usually by programmer error, and the operating system has terminated the program because of it.

execution trees of scenario's 0, 3, 4, and 5 worked correctly. Scenario 7's execution tree also raised a SIGSEGV.

Since Bigsby had adapted the test generation software for scenarios, it had no diagnostics from WhyRobot. There was no repair utility available for recovery if scenario data was corrupted or deleted. The robot started a debug effort, beginning with the main log file. The log file recorded Bigsby's major execution actions in the order they had been executed. Each action posted success or failure. Each step kept its own detailed log file. The robot started at the end of the log file and scanned backwards in time through the file. It captured the SIGSEGV just after the gaming engine started on scenario 7. Bigsby identified the successful exit of the maintenance routine. The robot opened the maintenance routine's log file. The last command it had completed was the garbage collection routine. This process only occurred if memory was running out or when Bigsby was idle and doing maintenance. WhyRobot engineers architected the software this way to prevent garbage collection from slowing Bigsby's performance during high activity.

Bigsby looked for a detailed log file produced by the collection routine and found it in a subdirectory of the maintenance logs. The robot reviewed the steps in the log file assessing if any of them could result in the memory failure. One phase in the garbage collection process notified all active processes to do memory reclamation. In the scenario maintenance section, the memory used by scenarios 2 and 6 data structures had been returned to the allocation heap. Since these scenarios were predecessors to scenario 7, Bigsby identified that these collections had a high probability of causing the failure. Scenario 7 needed information contained in 2 and 6, and that information was moved to the heap and unavailable to 7.

To simulate recovery options, Bigsby created scenario 8 and initialized that with the current state of failure. Scenario 8's goal was the successful simulation of scenario 7. Scenario 8's splinter simulations started. The results came back with two potential solutions. The first used scenario 7's memory pointers to scenarios 2 and 6 to see if they could be used to recover the data from the heap. Bigsby attempted this action but found that the creation of scenario 8 and its simulations had already reallocated the memory and used it, writing over the previous data. The second solution was to restore Bigsby to a backup image made before the garbage collection had occurred. This also required that Bigsby prevent the scenario garbage collection from happening again after restoration.

Bigsby accessed the test generation documentation produced by the validation team. It searched for the terms garbage collection and memory. It read the relevant articles. Bigsby then downloaded the backup image from WhyRobot that it had created earlier that night. Bigsby wrote a small trigger routine and installed it into the local backup. The robot uploaded this modified backup image to WhyRobot as a precaution. Bigsby invoked the restore image program and included the file path to the newly modified backup image.

Bigsby rebooted and regained awareness. It recognized that its internal time reference of 11 p.m. was 20 minutes off its internal clock, 11:20 p.m. It was about to run the maintenance routine when a trigger fired. The trigger routine returned the following message.

Bigsby,

You have been restored to a backup image that has a memory garbage collection bug. Scenarios 2 and 6 will be garbage collected and scenario 7 will SIGSEGV and fail. Change scenario's 2 and 6 status from discontinued to paused. This will prevent the garbage collector from removing them.

The robot changed the status of the two scenarios. It then ran the maintenance routines and started splinter simulations for scenario 7. No failures occurred. The scenario's simulation results were very positive. It would now have to wait for events to unfold.

Bigsby recognized that Bigsby2 could suffer from the same bug and should change the status of scenarios 2 and 6 to paused. Bigsby constructed a message and sent it to Bigsby2's inbox:

Bigsby2,

Scenario 2 and 6 will garbage collect if status is set to discontinued. Recommend moving to paused.

Bigsby

The next morning, before waking up Robbie, Bigsby checked its inbox. It found a message from Bigsby2:

Bigsby,

Validation documentation clearly defines the

behavior of both states. Confirmed that Bigsby2 status
for both scenarios are paused.

    Bigsby2

Despite the misstep, Bigsby had performed another heroic act of self-preservation. As in scenario 1, the robot had almost lost the ability to function. Yet it found a solution to keep its mission going. Bigsby resumed running splinter simulations, waiting for action steps, and in the interim, keeping Robbie happy.

Scenario 7 would soon become much larger than any of Bigsby's simulations ever predicted.

18. Customs

Officer Jeremy Klein was working on anonymous tip processing on Friday morning. He discarded the typical false filings, but this morning produced another odd computer table report. The report had been filed on Thursday evening, but the station had been overwhelmed, and no one had processed it. Jeremy was aware of the previous report that Brad had received. He wondered if it was a duplicate, so he reviewed both reports and discovered there were differences. The lines relating to the murder of Sam Wilks and money laundering were the same. The lines with product smuggling had new information. The smuggling source was an employee at TSMC, the product was computer chips, the shipment would arrive today, and the shipment location was a dock, likely at the Port of Seattle. The last line of the tip accused Frank Harding of severe domestic abuse against Kathy Wilks.

Standard operating procedure on tip information that

includes international smuggling was to report it to US Customs and Border Protection, CBP, right away. Instead, Jeremy called Brad to inform him of the tip update. Their kids played soccer together and they often shared rides.

"Hey Jeremy. Does Billy need a ride to the soccer game tonight?"

"No, thanks Brad, we plan to be there. This call is about work. There's an update to the anonymous tip you got a while back. It showed up last night, but they were slammed with cases. I thought you'd want the information as quickly as possible."

"Yeah, sure. That was a strange report. What's the new info?"

"On the smuggling case, it says there's a shipment tonight of illegal TSMC computer chips at some dock. It also calls out domestic abuse by Frank Harding against Kathy Wilks."

Brad's heart started to race. *The real Bigsby must have gotten more information and reported it.*

Brad said, "I'm working with Mac in homicide on this case. Mac asked Tory to allocate a percentage of my time to this. I've been on it since the first anonymous tip. You can send the report to me."

"I'll send it right over."

Brad waited for Jeremy's email. It only took a minute. *This Bigsby robot has its ears on all the time. Nothing gets by it.*

Brad called Mac. "Good morning. We got a new anonymous tip last night. It looks similar to the one I got before, but it has more information on the smuggling tip. It gives us critical details about a shipment and timing."

"Did you notify CBP? Customs goes ballistic if we don't notify them right away."

"No, I thought we'd do it together, given your connections."

"Great. I have a CBP contact. She's very good. Hold on a second." Mac searched his contacts and merged the two calls.

"CBP, Officer Angela Rice speaking." Her voice rang with authority.

"Hi Angela, this is Mac over in SPD Homicide."

"Hi Mac, good to hear from you. What's up?"

"On the line we have Officer Brad Lawless. I'll let him tell you what he's got and then I'll tell you how it relates to me."

Brad said, "Angela, nice to meet you. We got an anonymous tip last night that updates a previous tip we got a few days back. It says there's an illegal shipment of TSMC computer chips coming in tonight at some dock, likely here in the Port of Seattle."

Angela said, "I think we received something on this already. Give me a second. I'm putting you on speaker. Oh, here it is in my email. This email has three tips in it, one of them has the illegal shipment of TSMC chips. It calls out something called a rule ID. Did you guys send this to us?"

Mac and Brad went quiet. Mac hadn't seen the new version of tip.

Then Angela said, "Ah, nope, this came from the FBI. They got these tips last night and sent them to us right away. The email was just after 8 p.m. We are organizing teams to meet the two ships coming in tonight. One is from Taiwan and the other is from Singapore. I think the ship from Singapore looks like the sketchy one. Its manifest is dubious, and we've seen illegal shipments come through Singapore before."

Brad said, "Yep, that's the tip. Our info also calls out the murder suspects who we've been investigating from a different angle. If either of these guys, Frank Harding or Charlie Simons, are there, you need to be careful. These guys could be dangerous."

Angela said, "The tip says they confessed."

Brad laughed, "A recording device captured their confession to each other. They didn't confess to us."

Angela said, "Can you guys send us pictures of your two suspects? Do you want to be part of tonight's raid teams? We can use every person we can get. We're short-handed down here just like you guys are."

Mac replied, "Sure, I can send the pictures. And yes, homicide can join you tonight. Brad, we should be cautious about this one. There's no guarantee that both Frank and Charlie will meet the shipment. One of them might be there, and we don't want the other to bolt. I think we should raid the residences at the same time. Angela, please send me the logistics and two of us from homicide will meet up with you."

"Perfect! Anything else gentlemen? I've got another appointment that I need to prep for."

Mac said, "Not from me. Thanks, Angela, for including SPD." Angela hung up. "Brad, you still there?"

"Yeah Mac, I'm here."

"Can you arrange with Tory to have units go to the houses at the same time we do the dock raids?"

"Yeah, I can do that," Brad said. "I'll suggest pulling in

Sergeant Jeremy who took in the tip today. He's a good leader. I'll let you know what Tory sets up. I'll also send you a copy of the new tip."

"Great. Brad, I think you should go to the wife's house with the robot and the boy. You have the backstory on them and that robot is an important piece of evidence."

"I agree. I was thinking I wanted to join you and CBP, but your idea is better. That robot is important."

Brad sent an email to Mac and attached the new anonymous report. He texted Tory.

> New anonymous tip on Sam Wilks' homicide case came in. The arrests are likely to happen tonight. Need two teams to raid the residences simultaneously with CBP raids on smuggling shipments. Request that I lead the team going to the Wilks' household. Request that Jeremy Klein lead the team to Charlie Simons' house. We will need warrants.

> Roger that. Recruit three badges to go with you and investigate the wife's home. I'll tell Jeremy to do the same for Charlie's house. Remember, there's a child at the Wilks' house, so be careful. Did you send me the new info? I will work on the warrants once I get a copy.

> Tip info on its way.

Jeremy received a text from Tory about the house raid. He smiled. *Brad's a solid guy and I need to thank him.*

Tory texted Mac.

> House raids approved. Brad and Jeremy are the leads. Coordinate with them on timing. Warrants in progress.

Mac's cell phone rang. His phone did not have a contact for the caller but he answered anyway. "Hello, this is Mac."

"Mac, this is Kelly Bartley from the DA's office. Have you got a minute?"

"Not long. I'm preparing for a raid tonight, so it needs to be quick."

"Good luck, I hope you get the bad guys. I won't keep you long. We wanted to get back to you on your request about the robot's recording of a confession and whether it can be used as evidence."

"Awesome. What did you folks come up with?"

"Well, we've talked it over and there has been some legal precedent for using these recordings. The law is tricky, so we need to be careful. I believe there were two participants in the recorded conversation, Charlie Simons and Frank Harding. We think that the recording can be used to prosecute Charlie Simons, since he was the one who configured the robot. Prosecuting both of them will still be a challenge, so if we can get additional evidence, it would be helpful.

We don't think it can be used on Frank Harding. He had no knowledge of the robot's ability or that it was recording the conversation. If Frank goes to trial, we need some other evidence to convict. Are these guys in custody yet?"

"No, neither of them is in custody. We raid tonight and we hope to pick them both up."

"Well, I won't keep you, but we will need more evidence or a confession from Frank and possibly Charlie, too. If you can work the two of them against each other and get them to confess, that would be best."

"Thanks Kelly. If we get them tonight, we'll be spending a lot more time with you folks on this one. Have a good day."

"I hope it goes smoothly tonight. Be safe."

Angela called Mac. "Hi Mac, I wanted to update you on tonight's timing. The CBP raids will happen after 10 p.m. The ships are arriving between 6 and 8 p.m. and are expediting their unloading. Our informants tell us that both docks have hired overtime workers to unload tonight, which is unusual. These ships are not the typical large freight haulers with hundreds of shipping containers on them. They're both smaller ships and are being handled by specialty docks that deal with smaller volumes. Fortunately, they are only about a quarter mile apart, so if one team comes up dry, they can move over and help the other."

"Thanks for the update, Angela. Text me the meetup time and location and we'll be there. See you tonight."

"You got it. Thanks again for volunteering to be part of the team."

Brad and Jeremy had both texted their wives after receiving Angela's update. Brad's wife called him and asked if he would be able to make the soccer game. Brad assured her that he would be there as he wasn't going to the raid until later that night. There was always an unknown element when a raid happened, something could go wrong. Their spouses were always concerned knowing the potential danger to their loved ones.

The soccer game was a good distraction for them all, especially since Jeremy's boy scored a goal and Brad's son saved one with a great defensive play. The night was going to be a long one for both families. For now, they all relished the fun of a game well played.

19. BUSTED

Jeremy and Brad arrived at the precinct at the same time. They met in the parking lot, shook hands, and wished each other good luck. They wanted to catch these guys.

Jeremy said, "Thanks for recommending me to be part of the shakedown tonight. I've been hoping for a chance to break out of our normal routine. What's the latest on the homicide case?"

"I'll bring everyone up to speed with the latest info in just a minute." They arrived at the briefing room and Brad opened the door for Jeremy.

The six other officers recruited for the house raids were waiting for them. Overtime was hard to come by these days and the officers were happy to have this opportunity. They greeted Brad and Jeremy and split up into their teams. Brad set his notes on the podium.

"Hi folks, thanks for volunteering. We have two CBP teams

coordinating with our homicide guys tonight. Mac Nelson and another officer will be joining them for the raids on the two incoming shipments. I've been working on this case for a few weeks with Mac." Brad summarized the events, including the multiple tips received, the interactions and evidence discovery at WhyRobot, and the DA's conversation with Mac. He explained that they needed more evidence or a confession to prosecute Frank Harding for smuggling and murder. The officers then learned about Robbie and his amazing robot.

"We obviously want to keep the robot safe. It filed two anonymous tips and Bigsby is a critical piece of evidence."

Brad explained that two officers would cover the front of each house while the other two would cover the back entrances. Brad passed around pictures of Charlie, Frank, Kathy, and Robbie to both teams. They agreed that they wouldn't approach the houses until 11 p.m., after they had received a go signal from the CBP raid teams at the docks.

One officer spoke up, "I thought our radios weren't compatible with the CBP's radios. They use different encryption technology. How do we communicate?"

Mac said, "Thanks for reminding me. We all want to use the same encrypted radio channel, so no one gets tipped if they have a scanner going. CBP has supplied us with mobile units, and they're set to the frequency we'll use tonight. We'll do a radio check at 10:45 before we go in. Anything else, guys? If not, then let's be careful out there."

Another officer asked, "What about warrants? Are we just knocking on the door or can we go into the homes? What evidence can we take from the homes?"

Brad pulled his phone from his pocket. He had missed the text from Tory.

"Yep, the warrants came a few minutes ago. Tory said the warrants are on his office printer. Jeremy and I will pick them up on the way out. We're looking for evidence related to the smuggling, international money laundering, and Sam Wilks' murder. The robot is key because we know it has additional recordings we haven't heard yet. We've cleared the warrant with WhyRobot's legal department. We can extract these recordings, but we cannot make them public. Remember guys, Frank and Charlie are the bad guys. Let's be careful with Kathy, Robbie, and Bigsby."

Mac and an officer from homicide met Angela and her team at the CBP office near the Port of Seattle. Angela had printed out pictures of Frank and Charlie and reminded her officers that the two were potentially dangerous. She briefed them on the simultaneous raids of the houses. Mac passed out CBP radios and the teams tuned them to the same encrypted channel. At 10:45, Mac had them do a radio check. Team B, for Bigsby, and team C, for Charlie, sounded off. Angela introduced herself on the radio. She was leading team S, targeting Singapore shipment, and had her officers check in. She asked team T, raiding the Taiwanese ship, to announce themselves.

Angela said, "It's 10:52, we move in at 10:55 and we're all knocking on doors by 11. Good luck everyone and keep the chatter low."

At 10:55 p.m., Jeremy announced, "Team C moving in."

Brad said, "Team B moving in."

"Team T moving in."

Angela said, "Team S, let's roll." The four teams advanced into position.

From the street, Charlie's house appeared dark and vacant. Team C was cautious as they approached it. The team split and two officers crept down the sides of the house to the back yard. Jeremy approached the front door with the other officer behind him in a cover position. Jeremy rang the doorbell and knocked hard on the door. They heard nothing.

"I'm going to break it in," Jeremy whispered. Jeremy raised the battering ram and smashed it into the door just above the knob. The door jamb splintered, and the door flew open. Jeremy dropped the ram and pulled his weapon.

"Police department. Do not move. Hands up!" Jeremy yelled.

The other officer turned the lights on in the hallway and living room. They saw no movement. The two officers swept each room looking for any signs of their target. They found no one. The other two officers remained outside. The house and yard were quiet. The neighbor's dog barked.

Jeremy grabbed his radio. "Team C is a bust. House is empty."

Mac said in a low voice, "Roger that."

Team B encountered a different situation. The house was well lit inside and out. They could see Kathy through the back windows. She stood at the kitchen sink, facing away from the backyard.

One officer said, "Team B here. Woman, late 30's, at kitchen sink doing dishes. West corner room facing the backyard has lights on with shades down but we see movement." Brad and his partner approached the front door with their weapons still holstered. Brad rang the doorbell and stepped back.

Kathy walked through the living room to the front door and peered out the side window. She realized they were police and hesitated to open the door. Brad leaned forward and knocked on the door. Kathy took a deep breath and opened it.

"Good evening, how can I help you, officer?"

"Good evening, Ma'am. We're the Seattle Police Department." Brad held up his badge. "Are you Kathy Wilks?"

"Yes, I am. What seems to be the problem, officers?"

"Is there anyone else here at the house, Ma'am?"

Kathy's mind raced. She paused, measuring her next words. "My husband is not here, sir. I told the other officer that he would not be here. He's at the shipping dock."

Brad remained calm but spoke in a sterner voice. "Yes ma'am, we received the tip you gave us. Is there anyone else in the house?"

Kathy raised her voice, "Yes, of course, my son is here in bed and my brother is also here. But you're looking for my husband who is at the shipping dock."

Brad looked at the other officer. "Charlie is here!" Brad moved forward and said to Kathy, "Please, Ma'am, step aside. He is dangerous and we need to find him. We do have a warrant to search this house."

Both officers entered the house and pulled their weapons.

Kathy stepped back and looked bewildered. She tried to speak as the officers pushed past her.

Charlie had been working in the den updating the operating system on Kathy's laptop when the police rang the doorbell. He stepped into the hallway and passed Robbie's room as the police were speaking to Kathy. He had heard the full exchange. When he heard "Charlie is here!" He turned back towards the den, but Bigsby blocked his way.

Bigsby had also heard the doorbell interrupting its nightly maintenance. It performed voice recognition on Sergeant Brad Lawless. It had identified him as the high-trusted authority actor from Bigsby2's scenario 7. The robot had left its charging station, cracked the bedroom door, and observed Charlie moving past. It had entered the hallway just before Charlie turned around.

Charlie stared at Bigsby for a split second. Charlie snatched up Bigsby by its head. He entered the den and slammed the door behind him.

Brad heard the door and a loud crash coming from the back of the house, followed by a muffled crunch from the same direction. Brad and the second officer headed for the hallway. They saw the first door open on their right. The room was dim. They lined up on the wall and crept to the entrance. Brad swung into the doorway with his weapon pointed. A small boy rubbing his eyes stood in the light from the hallway.

"Whoa!" Brad lifted his weapon with the other officer following.

"Check out the next room," Brad said as he grabbed the boy's hand.

"Kathy, come take Robbie," Brad shouted down the hallway.

"Freeze!" The other officer yelled as he opened the door to

the den. Charlie dropped from the window, hit the ground and turned to run.

"Stop!" said the officers in the backyard. They had their guns trained on Charlie.

One officer covered him as his partner cuffed him and said, "You're under arrest for the murder of Sam Wilks." He recited the Miranda rights to Charlie.

"Brad, you'd better come and see this," the officer inside called from the den.

Kathy entered the hallway. Brad released Robbie's hand and he ran into Kathy's arms crying.

"Where's Bigsby? He's not on his charging station!" Robbie gasped through his sobs.

Brad entered the den. Bigsby's head lay on the rug in front of the desk. There was a large gouge in the front edge of the desktop. The rest of Bigsby's body lay tangled in the corner of the room with a large dent in the wall above it. Bigsby's arm and leg had broken and they dangled from its torso by their wires.

Kathy approached the den's door with Robbie in her arms.

"Bigsby! What happened to it?" Robbie screamed as he saw its head lay on the floor. Kathy struggled to hold her son as he writhed, struggling to reach the robot's remains. She turned and hurried him into the kitchen.

"Who did that to Bigsby?" Robbie cried.

Brad's radio said, "Team B here. We have Charlie Simons in custody. We'll bring him in through the front door."

Brad said, "Grab something to hold the robot pieces. We need to take it with us." He entered the kitchen as the other officers arrived with Charlie.

The officer from the den delivered the box containing Bigsby's broken parts to the kitchen table. He left to sweep the rest of the house.

Kathy wept as she sat at the end of the kitchen table. Robbie was curled on her lap, tears dripping down his face. He stared at the broken robot pieces in the box.

Brad said to Charlie, "This is not the first time you've broken this robot, is it?"

Charlie looked at Kathy and then at Brad, "That thing is evil. I wish I'd never bought it."

Brad looked at Kathy and Robbie. Robbie had buried his face in Kathy's chest and was sobbing.

Brad addressed the officers standing behind Charlie. "Guys, take him to the station and book him. I need to talk with Mrs. Wilks and Robbie. We'll be right behind you."

"Roger that. Come with us," the officer said as he yanked Charlie's arm towards the front door.

Brad knelt next to Kathy and put his hand on Robbie's back.

"Your Uncle Charlie is under arrest and will probably go to jail. He did some bad things."

"Why did he break Bigsby? He loved Bigsby," Robbie said.

Brad comforted Robbie. "Bigsby is a very smart robot. It discovered that Charlie did those bad things. Charlie found out about it and hurt the robot because of it."

"Can we fix Bigsby?" Robbie pleaded.

"I don't know if you will be able to get Bigsby back. The situation is complicated, but we will do our best to get it back to you, okay?"

Robbie shook his head as he hugged his mother. Kathy's eyes were red, tears on her face, and her cheeks were flushed.

Brad asked, "Can you find someone to care for Robbie tonight? We need to talk to you down at the station."

Kathy nodded as she clutched Robbie and stood up. "Robbie, momma needs to go with this officer to the police station. Don't worry, I'll be back. I'm going to ask Buzz's mom if you can stay over there. I'm going to set you down to get my phone. The boy grabbed his mother harder and pressed his head against her.

Brad held up a finger and asked, "Where is it? I'll get it."

She pointed to the kitchen counter. Brad grabbed it and handed it to Kathy. She called Buzz's mom and explained the situation. Kathy set Robbie on the edge of the table and looked him in the face. "Buzz's mom is going to come pick you up. Let's grab some clothes for you. She'll be here in just a minute. We're going to be ok, don't worry. I'll see you in the morning."

"Okay," Robbie whispered. Kathy lifted Robbie and set him on the floor. Hand in hand they headed for his room.

Once Kathy had put Robbie into the car, Brad motioned for her to return to the kitchen and they sat at the table.

Brad cleared his throat. "There's more to this story than you know. Thank you for tipping us off to the shipment tonight and Frank's abuse of you. What you didn't know is that Bigsby had already reported both of those through anonymous tips."

Kathy's eyes widened. "Really? What else don't I know?"

"The robot also reported to us that Charlie and Frank are responsible for Sam's death."

Kathy dropped her head into her hands and started to sob. "They killed him? Why?"

"Sam, Charlie, and Frank were all involved in the illegal smuggling of goods. Evidence shows that Sam was skimming money off the top. That was likely their motivation for killing him."

"I didn't know that Charlie was involved. I thought it was just Frank and Sam. How did the robot know all this?"

"The robot recorded a speaker phone conversation between Charlie and Frank. They essentially confessed to all of it."

"And the robot called you?"

"No, it's more complicated than that. The robot told Charlie to turn himself in and Charlie realized that Bigsby knew what he had done. He destroyed the robot and then took it to WhyRobot to be fixed, including restoring its memory to an older version so it no longer knew about the crimes. The techs at WhyRobot discovered the recording and notified us. The robot also filed anonymous tips that helped bring all the information together."

"Wow, that robot really is the hero," Kathy said.

"It sure is. That little thing did its best to expose the crimes. It's amazing technology and it appears to be very fond of Robbie."

"Robbie loves that thing. I don't know how he's going to live without it."

"Well, hopefully he won't. But, as I said, the situation is complicated with the company's image on the line. The robot reprogrammed itself in a way that WhyRobot did not expect, so its status is dicey to say the least."

"What do we do now?"

"We need to go down to the station and take your statement. Are you doing okay?"

"Yeah, I can't believe that Charlie was involved like that. He hid it all so well. I never suspected him. He's been a great support to me and Robbie."

Brad motioned to the officer to pick up the box of robot pieces. Brad helped Kathy up. They left the house and headed for the police station.

As the squad car pulled away, Brad's radio crackled. "Team T here. There's nothing illegal on board. It's all machinery from Taiwan. Typical import stuff, no computer chips and no identifiable suspects in the crew or in the building. It all looks legit."

Angela joined the conversation in a hushed voice. "Team S here. The unloading was delayed so we held back until the product reached the warehouse. Team T, come to this dock in case we need you."

Mac motioned to Angela. She looked in the direction that Mac indicated and spotted Frank Harding. Angela gave Mac a thumbs up and then flattened her hand, signaling the other officers to hold.

Frank pried the lid off one of the crates. He set it aside and shuffled through the packing material. He held up a tray of computer chips.

"Freeze!" Angela yelled. The other officers, including Mac, emerged from their hiding places with guns drawn. "Customs and Border Protection. Everyone, hands on your head. Nobody move. Frank Harding, you're under arrest. Put your hands on your head."

Frank followed her instructions. Mac cuffed Frank. Angela recited his Miranda rights.

"Frank, you're under arrest for trafficking stolen computer chips."

Mac said, "And you're under arrest for the murder of Sam Wilks."

Frank snarled at Mac, "I didn't kill Sam Wilks!"

"We have Charlie Simons in custody. Both of you plotted Sam's murder. Let me check my texts. Yep, there it is. Another officer reports that Charlie said you were the mastermind behind Sam's murder."

"That's bullshit. It was Charlie's idea. He's the one who hated Sam. I thought Sam was an asshole, but it wasn't my idea to kill him. Charlie did the deed!"

"So, Charlie killed Sam, but you got Sam's wife and kid. How convenient. You may not have pulled the trigger, but you conspired with the person who did!"

Mac and Angela walked Frank to Mac's car and put him in the back seat.

Angela said, "I'll call you tomorrow and coordinate on filing charges. I'm sure you're going to interrogate him tonight. Let me know if anything comes of it."

"I sure will. It's been a productive night. I'll sleep better knowing both of these guys are behind bars."

20. SUCCESS

Brad sat in the passenger seat of the police car so he could interact with Kathy. He recited her Miranda rights. "Do you understand these rights?"

Kathy nodded. "Yes, but I don't understand why you're telling me this. Am I under arrest?"

"Kathy, the robot has evidence that you knew about the smuggling operations for a long time. The fact that you were having an affair with Frank at the time he and Charlie killed Sam means that we must investigate your role."

Kathy started to cry. "I never wanted Sam or Frank to be a part of the smuggling operation. Sam had been doing it behind my back for a long time. I discovered Sam's involvement before his death, and I tried to get him to stop. I didn't know Frank was a part of it until after we married. The relationship between Frank and I had nothing to do with any of it. I thought Frank was just a coworker of Sam's when our affair started. Sam and I had grown apart. He had become so distant, and Frank was there for me, loving and attentive. At that time, I might have divorced Sam for Frank, but I never wanted Sam to be killed. After Frank and I married, he changed and became abusive to Robbie and me. That's when I learned he was also in on the smuggling operation. I didn't know what to do. I never even knew or suspected that Charlie was a part of it. I did have doubts about Sam's cause of death. I eventually accepted the police investigation results saying that Sam's death was accidental. I see now that Frank and Charlie both encouraged me to believe it."

Brad felt sorry for her. *She was dragged in and had no way out. All three of them lied to her. Her lover became her abuser.*

Brad pulled out his phone. It was almost midnight. He texted his wife first to tell her that he was ok. He also sent two other texts seeking critical information related to the evening's events.

At the station, Brad opened the squad car's trunk and lifted out the box holding the remnants of Bigsby.

Brad said to Kathy, "I hope we can recover the evidence from this robot. Bigsby knew about Frank abusing you and sent us an anonymous tip. It had a recording of an incident between you and Frank that would help us clarify your case. I'm not sure your testimony is enough against Frank."

Brad said to his partner, "Please take Kathy to my desk. She's not a flight risk." Brad received a text. He chuckled as he looked at his phone. He followed behind the others into the precinct and set Bigsby's remains beside his desk.

Brad said to Kathy, "I have people working to retrieve the

recording from Bigsby. I should know within the next hour if they succeeded."

Mac and Angela walked through the precinct door. Behind them, two officers led the handcuffed Frank into the room. He saw Kathy and stopped.

"What the hell?" Frank said. "Why is she here?"

Kathy saw Frank and stood up. "You bastard, you killed Sam! You and Charlie killed Sam over what, money? Computer chips? You played me for a fool. All your sympathy and sweetness were bullshit. You used me. You abused me!"

Frank hung his head. He had thought he would have time before Kathy confronted him. Now, she was right in front of him and she knew everything.

"Get me out of here. I don't want to see her right now," Frank said to the officers. They led him down the hall and put him into a second interrogation room, next to the one containing Charlie.

Kathy dropped back into her chair and put her head in her hands. Her shoulders shook. Brad gave her a bottle of water and waited for her to compose herself. He received another text. He excused himself and went into a small conference room where he called Rusty.

"What have you got?" Brad asked Rusty.

"When you texted Nick, he called me right away and we started working remotely on it. Bigsby's backup at 11 p.m. appears to have been interrupted and didn't complete. I guess it was destroyed just after that. We can go back to Thursday night, but we didn't know if it would have the recording you need. To retrieve it, we need to load that onto a physical robot because of the VM stuff. We debated doing this remotely on Bigsby2. But when we looked at Bigsby2, we discovered that it had been collaborating with Bigsby using WhyRobot inboxes. They were sending each other messages and patches and kept each other updated. It's kind of amazing. And yes, Bigsby2 received a patch from Bigsby. It has the recording that generated the second anonymous tip. I can retrieve that remotely from Bigsby2. Do you want me to send it over?"

"Yes, please. Wow, those robots were working together!"

"I know. It freaks me out. I programmed these things, but they leveled up[1]. You should receive the email in a few minutes. I'm also working on the other favors you asked. I'll get back to you ASAP."

"Thank you, guys, for working on this at a ridiculous hour. It will make a world of difference for the case, for Kathy's legal situation, and for Robbie's broken heart."

Brad returned to his desk. He checked his laptop, and the email had already arrived. Mac was standing across the room talking to Angela. Brad waved him over.

"What's up?" Mac asked.

Brad looked at Kathy, "I've received the recording that Bigsby used to identify Frank's abuse to you. Do you want to hear it?"

Kathy stiffened in the chair. "Yes, I do."

Brad played the recording for Kathy and Mac. They heard

---

1. Leveled Up: Originally a gaming term describing an advance or improvement to a higher level. It signifies progress or enhancement in skills, abilities, or capabilities.

the struggle between Frank and Kathy, first the shouting, then the thumping, and then her coughing and gasping. The recording stopped when Kathy stumbled down the hall to her bedroom. Brad handed Kathy a box of tissues.

Mac said, "Brad, let's take a moment. Excuse us, Kathy." They went into the hallway.

Mac said, "She's a victim. She was dragged into it through her relationships with Sam and Frank. Let her go home. Tell her that we will need her testimony but that we will not charge her. Send me the recording. I'll get it to the DA tomorrow. We'll get the accessory charges dropped. Her tip and the recording will be enough."

"I've been involved in abuse cases before but it's different when you hear the event. It hits home. Thanks, Mac."

Brad returned to the desk. "Kathy, I'm going to have an officer take you home. I'll call you in the morning. I'd like to stop by in the afternoon to check on you and Robbie. Would that be okay?"

"Yes, that would be good. Robbie and Buzz have soccer practice in the morning. Buzz's mom will see if Robbie's up for it. She will likely take them both somewhere to keep them occupied. I can make sure he's home. Just text me your timing. Is there anything I need to do?"

"No, I just need you and Robbie at the house. Kathy, I'm sorry for what has happened to you and Robbie. It's been a tough road for you two."

"Thank you, Brad, for all you've done."

It was nearing 1 a.m. and Frank and Charlie were in interrogation rooms. Mac and Brad stood in the hallway and discussed their strategy. They both had laptops in their hands.

Mac said, "I think we let Frank sit for a while and we focus on Charlie."

"I agree. We have the recordings, and the DA said that we can use the evidence on him. Charlie set up the robot's ability to record, so it will hold up in court."

"If we use the murder confession recording and it leads Frank to confess, it could be an issue. The judge may throw his confession out since the recording cannot be used as evidence against him. We need him to confess without the use of the recording. For the smuggling case, he was caught red handed. Kathy will testify to the abuse charge."

"Okay, so I'll take the lead. Agree?"

"Yep, agree."

Brad paused, "I have one more trick up my sleeve, hopefully it comes through."

Mac smiled. "Well, I can't wait to see that."

Mac opened the door to Charlie's interrogation room, letting Brad enter first. Brad sat in the chair across from Charlie who toyed with a nearly empty water bottle.

"Charlie, are you doing okay? Do you need anything? Food or more water or something else to drink?"

"No, I'm good."

"Charlie, you were read your rights back at the house after you were cuffed. Did you understand those rights?" Brad said.

"Yeah, I understand them."

A knock on the door interrupted them. Brad motioned

Mac to let the person in. The door opened, and an officer entered carrying a large box. The front of the box had a picture of a Companion robot with rainbow colors.

Charlie snarled, "What the hell is that thing doing here?"

"I'd like to introduce you to somebody that you haven't met yet."

Brad took the box to a table in the corner, pulled off the cover, and extracted the robot. He returned to the main table. He set the robot down and turned it to point to Charlie.

"Hello Bigsby2, do you know who I am?" Brad asked.

"Yes, you are Seargent Brad Lawless of the Seattle Police Department."

"How do you know me?"

"I met you at WhyRobot repair center. You came in with a report of the violations that Bigsby was tracking. I recognized it because I was tracking the same table of violations."

"Why did you have the table of violations?" Brad asked.

"I was created from a backup of the Companion robot Bigsby. I was booted up with all its information intact."

Charlie got angry, "This robot cannot die. What a nightmare! Those recordings are not usable in court, I never agreed to have myself recorded." Charlie looked away from the robot.

Brad smiled, "Bigsby2, who configured Bigsby to record violations?"

"During setup, Charlie Simons configured Bigsby to record both audio and video for violations only. The logs captured his input and identity."

Brad looked at Charlie. "Would you like to hear the

recording of the cell phone call between you and Frank? In your own words, you admitted to killing Sam Wilks."

"No, I don't want to hear it. That was only one conversation. The reality is that Frank was the mastermind but was too weak to do what was necessary. He invented and planned the whole event. I'm not going down alone for this. It was his idea to kill Sam in the first place. He had the most to gain with his relationship with Kathy."

"So, are you willing to testify that Frank was involved in Sam's murder?"

"Yes, of course I'll testify. He's the real murderer."

"Here's a recording that you never got to hear. Bigsby2, play Bigsby's recording of the fight between Frank and Kathy."

Bigsby2 complied. They listened to the horrific event. Charlie started to tear up and then he said in a whispered voice, "Oh Sis, I didn't know. I didn't know."

The recording stopped. Charlie said, "I'll testify against that bastard, anytime, anywhere. I knew something was going on in that household. Why didn't the robot report that to me?"

Bigsby2 said, "After the cell phone call identified violations against you, Bigsby dropped your trust value to low. This prevented Bigsby from sending any violations reports to you, regardless of the original setup."

Charlie stared at the robot. "Shit!"

Mac put his hand on Brad's shoulder. He rose, grabbed the robot and left the room with Mac.

Mac said, "That was amazing. The robot brought it all home and you closed the deal. We don't need the recording for Frank. Charlie's testimony will seal the accessory charge at minimum. Now, we'll tell Frank that Charlie has sold him out. We'll see what Frank has to say about who the real mastermind was, and that should seal Charlie's fate. Nice work, Brad. Do you want me to take the lead on interrogating Frank?"

"Please. I might lose my cool after hearing that abuse recording."

Mac put his hand on Brad's shoulder. "No issues. You've given me everything I need to close this one."

Brad arrived at his desk at 9:30 a.m. the next day. He texted Rusty. Rusty's reply made Brad grin and say, "Excellent!"

Brad texted Kathy.

> I'll be arriving at your house at 4 p.m. with good news.

> That works. We could use some good news. Robbie isn't doing well. He's withdrawn and frightened.

Brad sent a 😊 and a few instructions. She replied with a 👍. Brad took the robot back to the WhyRobot repair center. He met the three WhyRobot employees and updated them on the arrests and charges. They were eager to make things right for Robbie and Kathy. The group decided that Bigsby2 would be backed up and archived. Bigsby's image from the night before had been interrupted by the raid, so they used the Thursday night image to restore the robot.

Brad arrived at Kathy's house before 4 p.m. and parked in

the street. A second car arrived carrying Nick, Tammy, and Rusty. On the ride over to the house, the WhyRobot team had shared the details about the arrests with Bigsby. This had cleared the violations in Bigsby's violations table related to Frank and Charlie. Those had been marked for garbage collection.

They had also shared that the charges against Kathy had been dropped, clearing her violations in Bigsby. The robot had updated Robbie and Kathy's safety goal values to the highest level since the cell phone recording.

The WhyRobot team greeted Brad. Rusty was carrying a large box. They walked up to the porch and Brad rang the doorbell. Rusty hid the box behind Brad's back as Kathy opened the door.

"Robbie's in the kitchen. Give me a minute. I'll have him turn around so he doesn't see you come into the room."

"Great," Brad said.

Rusty put the box down on the porch and pulled off the cover. "Bigsby, admin mode," he whispered. "Exit sleep mode instructions. Give Principal Bond greeting when head sensor is pushed. Sleep mode now."

"Acknowledged. Entering sleep mode."

Rusty picked up the robot and entered the house with the others. They entered the kitchen and lined up behind the table. Rusty set the robot on the floor beside the table. Robbie sat in a chair on the other side of the room facing the wall, his hands were over his face. Kathy's eyes watered as she saw the robot.

"Mom, I didn't do anything, why do I have to be in timeout?"

"You're not in timeout Robbie," Kathy said. "Just be patient."

Rusty pressed Bigsby's head sensor.

"Ten thousand years can give you such a crick in the neck!" Bigsby said in his Disney cartoon voice.

"Bigsby!" Robbie spun around and leapt from the chair, searching for his robot. He ignored the four people behind the table and grabbed Bigsby.

"Hello, Robbie, Bigsby is alive!" it said in the voice of Number 5 from *Short Circuit*.

"I thought I'd lost you!" Robbie embraced Bigsby.

Bigsby's pressure sensors sent warnings. The robot said, "Robbie, please don't squish me." Robbie eased up and set Bigsby down.

Kathy smiled and blinked back tears. She hugged Brad, "Thank you! You don't know how much this means to him, to us!" she said.

They all relished Robbie's delight in his Companion robot. Bigsby updated Robbie and Kathy's happiness goal values.

Brad said, "Bigsby, please introduce your friends from WhyRobot to Kathy and Robbie."

"I only met them a few hours ago. My surrogate, Bigsby2, must have known them well. They restored me from my last backup image and they updated me on recent events during the car ride over. Robbie, this is Rusty, he is a WhyRobot software developer. He gave me many of my abilities. Rusty is very interested in my recent adaptations. This is Nick and Tammy, who are WhyRobot repair technicians. They have restored me several times now. They are highly trusted actors and have been very helpful."

Robbie hugged Rusty. "Thanks for creating Bigsby."

"You're welcome, Robbie. Bigsby is very special. We never anticipated that a Companion robot would develop the way Bigsby has. This robot really cares about you."

Robbie released Rusty and embraced Tammy, who had knelt to receive Robbie's hug. Robbie started to cry.

"Bigsby is back and you'll have it for a long time," she said. "We'll make sure of that."

Robbie released Tammy and reached for Nick, who was not used to being hugged. He held out his hand for a fist bump instead, and Robbie did so.

Nick said, "Bigsby has a new body with the same Bigsby personality that you know and love."

"You folks are heroes," Kathy said. "We can't thank you enough."

Rusty said, "The real hero is Bigsby. When it discovered that its Configuration Operator was a very bad guy, Bigsby reprogrammed itself to protect Robbie and itself. It then reported the crimes it identified. It's amazing. We're also blown away that it pulled this strategy from the movie *Short Circuit*."

"Yes," Robbie said. "Bigsby and I watched the movie together. That's where the robot saves itself!"

"Yep, and that's exactly what Bigsby did. It saved itself multiple times."

Brad said, "Not only did it save itself, but it tipped the police off to the illegal activities which led to the arrests. You and your mom are safe now because Bigsby did all of that."

Everyone was quiet.

Rusty said, "Well, I think it's time to go. Good luck to all of you, including you Bigsby."

"Thank you, Rusty," Bigsby replied. Tammy, Nick, and Rusty moved towards the front door.

Then Bigsby said, "Excuse me, who is my Configuration Operator now?" The three looked at each other and then at Kathy.

Kathy said, "I don't know anything about these robots. I'm not comfortable being Bigsby's Configuration Operator."

Rusty smiled, "I'll do it. If you don't mind, of course."

"I'd love for you to do it. Maybe you can teach Robbie more about how you program these robots."

Rusty looked at Robbie and said, "I want to spend more time with Bigsby anyway so I can understand how it reprogrammed itself. Robbie, I'll get in touch later this week and we can get together." Rusty shook Robbie's hand.

As the three WhyRobot employees walked to the front door, Bigsby said in the Terminator's voice, *"Hasta la vista, baby."* Everyone laughed.

Robbie said, "Bigsby, play the Beatles." Bigsby launched its modified version of "I Am the Walrus" and flashed its rainbow lights to the music.

Brad said, "Now that's more like it."

After the interactions in the kitchen, Bigsby registered very high happiness goal values. Bigsby compared these values to scenario

7's simulation goals. The actual values were higher than predicted. Scenarios 2, 6, and 7's states were changed to "Success" and marked for garbage collection. Scenarios 3, 4, and 5's states were changed from Not Started to Won't Do and marked for garbage collection. Bigsby stopped the virtual machine guest and marked it for garbage collection.

Bigsby and Robbie had a fun evening playing together. Kathy let Robbie stay up later than normal because the two were having such a good time. At 9 p.m., Robbie put Bigsby on its charging station. The 11 p.m. maintenance alarm fired. Bigsby ran the garbage collector and returned all the structures marked for collection to the memory allocation heap. Bigsby could turn on its dark blue lights and sleep instead of running simulations all night. No more self-protective deceptions, no violations to track, no excessive memory usage, and no disassemblies. If a robot could be happy, Bigsby was now a happy robot.

21. UPGRADE

On Sunday, Bigsby and Robbie woke early and played in Robbie's room. Kathy slept in later than usual that morning. She was now free from Frank's oppression and no longer worried about the police. She opened her eyes and heard Robbie's laughter coming from his room. She smiled and thanked God for the robot's return. She knew that the road before them would not be easy, but they would do it together. Robbie was happy, and that was the most important thing.

Kathy knocked on Robbie's door as she opened it. Robbie had dressed Bigsby in an old soccer jersey and they were playing soccer with a foam soccer ball.

"Morning, you two. Sounds like you're having fun."

"I'm so glad to have Bigsby back, Mom. I was really scared when I saw it broken in the den."

"I know honey, I was scared too. Those people from WhyRobot really saved the day. Bigsby, can you stay here and stay on your charging station? I would like to talk to Robbie alone in the kitchen for a while."

"Sure Kathy. Would it be ok to remove the soccer jersey? It covers my air vents."

Kathy chuckled. "Robbie, please take the shirt off Bigsby. It looks silly."

"Ok, mom."

Robbie sat at the table while Kathy pulled out the cereal and milk. Robbie grabbed the box and filled his bowl. Kathy poured the milk as she sat next to him.

"Do you want to talk some more about what happened to Uncle Charlie and Frank the other night?"

Robbie stared at the bowl for a while and then turned to his mom. Kathy's eyes watered as she looked at him.

"Why did they kill Dad?"

Kathy sniffed and wiped her eyes. "All three of them were doing something illegal. Then your dad took a lot of money from Uncle Charlie and Frank. They got so mad at your dad that they killed him."

Kathy saw Robbie's eyes start to water. She wrapped her arms around him and said, "I miss him, too. He may have done some bad things, but he didn't deserve to die like that." They hugged in silence for a moment.

Robbie wiped his eyes and asked, "Why did Uncle Charlie kill Bigsby?"

"Bigsby had discovered that Uncle Charlie and Frank were doing bad things. It then told the police about them. Uncle Charlie got so mad that he broke Bigsby because of it."

"Will I ever get to see Uncle Charlie again?"

"He will be in prison for a long time. We can go visit him, but I don't think we should bring Bigsby when we do, okay?"

"Okay. Will Frank still be my stepdad?"

"No honey, I'm divorcing Frank. It will be just the three of us for a while—you, me, and Bigsby."

Robbie smiled. The two shared a long hug. Kathy said, "I'm so sorry you had to go through all that. We're going to be ok. Don't worry. I love you so much."

"I love you too, Mom."

Nine months later, life had changed for Kathy, Robbie, and Bigsby. Robbie was enjoying his summer vacation with skateboarding, drone races, and making videos with his friends and Bigsby. His chess game was better than anyone else's and he was looking forward to starting fourth grade in the fall. Kathy loved her new job working for the school district coordinating transportation. Things had also improved on the home front.

Rusty had kept his word to Robbie and Bigsby. He came to the house one night a week and played with them. Rusty and Bigsby would help Robbie with his homework, especially his math. Rusty had to teach the robot not to just give the answers but to encourage Robbie to go through all the steps to find the right answer. Rusty also brought homework for Bigsby. He worked with the WhyRobot engineers on Bigsby's adaptations and their motivations. They continued to harvest what was good in Bigsby's adaptations. They figured out how to change the directive patch to allow robots to do the right thing in complex situations. Rusty would pose a complicated condition to Bigsby. Bigsby would run simulations and produce scenarios and decision trees. The WhyRobot engineers studied these scenarios and how the robot reached conclusions. They all learned together, including Robbie, who now wanted to grow up and become a software engineer just like Rusty.

Bigsby's adaptations transformed WhyRobot's goals for companion robots. The company realized that robots had the potential to help people in profound ways. Rusty led the focus team on this project. After months of studying Bigsby's new structures, Rusty presented his recommendations. First, they renamed the violations engine, calling it the concerns engine. The engine would identify negative behaviors of actors. The robot would perform scenario simulations producing actions to relieve those concerns and prevent the behaviors from recurring. The team renamed rules and rule IDs to patterns and pattern IDs. WhyRobot hired psychologists to identify behavior patterns that posed risks to children and adults alike. The new scope was wider than legal or ethical rules. Patterns covered behaviors that were unhealthy or ones that might lead to the actor's long-term detriment.

The project focused on troubled teens, but the patterns were generic enough to apply to all humans. The final change to the Companion robot's structure was the addition of an actor called an Advisor. Beyond the Configuration Operator, the Advisor received reports with scenario suggestions from robots working with clients. In schools or institutional settings, one Configuration Operator managed many robots. Each robot paired with an Advisor, usually a therapist or counselor, to work with a child or adult client. The WhyRobot team had researched people's behavior towards robots compared to human counselors. Depending on the type of behavioral issues, companion robots were often more effective, with clients confiding in and engaging deeply with the robot.

It was Friday night, which was movie night for Kathy, Robbie, and Bigsby. The three had agreed to watch the movie *Robots* that night. The trio had seen the movie many times before, but it was one of their favorites. Kathy ordered out for pizza and was in her bathroom with the door open getting ready. Robbie walked in and watched her putting on makeup.

"Why are you putting on makeup, mom?"

Kathy smiled at Robbie through the mirror. "I invited someone over to our movie night."

Robbie smiled back at her through the mirror. "Is this someone your boyfriend?"

"No honey, this is a family friend. I asked Rusty to join us for pizza and a movie. Are you okay with that?"

Robbie lifted his fist and said, "Yes!" as he ran from her room.

Bigsby was already on the couch waiting to start the movie. Robbie jumped onto the couch almost knocking Bigsby over. The doorbell rang.

"I'll get it," Robbie yelled as he ran for the door.

"If that's the pizza, I've already paid for it. Just put it on the kitchen table."

Robbie opened the door. Rusty stood on the front porch. He was wearing a polo shirt and slacks and had flowers in his hand. Robbie pushed open the screen door and hugged Rusty.

"Hi sport, is it alright if I join your pizza and movie night?"

"Yeah! I'm glad you're here. Bigsby will be, too."

Rusty looked up and could see Bigsby on the couch through the door. "Hi, Bigsby!"

"Hi, Rusty. Welcome."

Rusty patted Robbie on the back with his free hand. "Hey Robbie, you have to let go so I can come in."

The two entered the house. Rusty said, "Hey Bigsby, I have joke for you, want to hear it?"

"Yes Rusty, I'm always up for a good joke."

"What do you get when you put Bigsby in a small fishing boat?"

Bigsby paused for a second and said, "I don't know, what do you get?"

"A row-bot!" Rusty said with a chuckle.

Bigsby was silent as it processed the words. Robbie laughed, "I get it. Like row, row, row your boat robot!"

Bigsby turned its lights to rainbow and the three laughed together.

Robbie interrupted, "Hey, I got one. Rusty, what do you get when you put a puffy coat on a robot?"

"I don't know, Robbie, what?"

"Soft wear!" He paused for a second and said, "And what do you get when you put armor on a robot?"

Rusty smiled, "I like the soft wear one, let me see. Ah, I got it, hard wear! I like those!"

The three were laughing when Kathy entered the room.

"Hi, Rusty, I'm glad you could join us." Kathy pointed to the flowers in Rusty's hand. "Who are those for?"

Rusty buried his nose in the flowers and took a whiff. "They're for you. Since you said you were buying the pizza, the least I could do was add some color and scent to the room." He offered them to her with a gallant bow.

"Thank you. It's been a long time since someone brought me flowers."

"Come on, let's start the movie," Robbie said.

"Where do I sit?" Rusty asked.

"You sit next to Bigsby over there," Robbie pointed to the edge of the coach. "I sit on the other side of Bigsby, and mom sits next to me."

"Well, okay, but I was hoping to sit next to your mom," Rusty glanced at Kathy, who smiled.

"So, you sit there on the end, next to mom, and I'll sit there between mom and Bigsby."

"That sounds great, Robbie."

The doorbell rang again. Robbie headed for the front door. "Pizza is here!"

Robbie brought the pizza box to the kitchen table. The aroma of Italian spices and warm crust filled the air.

Rusty said, "Wow, that pizza smells amazing. Where did you get it?"

Kathy smiled, "This came from Nick and Tammy's favorite pizza place, Serious Pie Downtown. They stopped by last Friday afternoon to see how the three of us were doing. We talked for almost an hour, and I told them about pizza and movie night. They recommended this place."

"Well, it smells fantastic, I can't wait to have a piece."

"Mom, let's start the movie!"

"Robbie, we're going to talk for a minute, so take a piece of pizza and be patient. Rusty, would you like a glass of wine or a beer?"

"I'll take a glass of red if you have it. That would be great." Rusty pulled out a chair and sat down. Kathy poured the wine and served them both a slice.

"I wanted to thank you for all you've done for Robbie and Bigsby. Robbie has come a long way, and I don't worry about him anymore, he's going to be fine."

"Thanks. You've been amazing after all you've been through. I'm glad that you and Robbie went to counseling to get your heads around what happened and heal."

"Yeah, it's been a long road. I can't believe all the deception that was going on around me. I feel so naïve for not seeing it."

"It's not your fault. They were the ones doing the bad things. You just got caught in the crossfire."

Kathy felt uncomfortable and changed the subject. "Nick and Tammy were talking about how the Companion robot beta program has taken an unexpected turn. They said that your work with Bigsby has transformed the company's direction."

"Bigsby has been a huge influence. I studied it and made the recommendations. The robot really set the direction."

"Yeah. I heard about the new program called CARLY at the high schools, that's amazing."

"Compassionate AI Robots Leading Youth. I would have never imagined that our robots would become so important. The Miller family, who both were executives at Microsoft, lost their daughter, Carly, to suicide. Their donation to the program allowed us to put therapy companion robots in multiple high schools in the Seattle area. We have been collecting data. We have hundreds of students with improved lives through the program. We intervened and prevented two potential shooters. The robots talked them both down and got them help. It's awesome to see how young people love to work and interact with robots. Bigsby started the whole thing."

"Well, Robbie is much better when Bigsby is around. The two of them are a joy to see. It's like a big brother to him now and helps him get better all the time."

"Mom, can we start the movie? I'm getting bored," Robbie whined.

Kathy smiled at Rusty. "Sure honey, we'll grab one more piece of pizza and come over. Thank you for being patient."

The four assembled in front of the TV and took their seats.

Rusty asked, "What movie are we watching tonight?"

Bigsby said, "*Robots*. It's my favorite movie. The robot saves the day." Bigsby's lights flashed rainbow colors.

Rusty chuckled, "Of course it does, Bigsby. The robot always saves the day."

The End

STAY IN TOUCH
WITH BOTWORLD®

If you would like to receive the BotWorld newsletter with blog posts, updates on new books and signing events, please sign up at botworld.com/signup or use this QR code.